MAR 10

THE HIGHLY
EFFECTIVE DETECTIVE
Plays the Fool

THE HIGHLY
EFFECTIVE DETECTIVE
Plays the Fool

RICHARD YANCEY

Minotaur Books

A Thomas Dunne Book
New York

This is a work of fiction. All of the characters, organizations, and events portrayed in this novel are either products of the author's imagination or are used fictitiously.

A THOMAS DUNNE BOOK FOR MINOTAUR BOOKS.
An imprint of St. Martin's Publishing Group.

www.thomasdunnebooks.com
www.minotaurbooks.com

Library of Congress Cataloging-in-Publication Data

Yancey, Richard.
    The highly effective detective plays the fool / Richard Yancey.—1st ed.
        p. cm.
    "A Thomas Dunne book."
    ISBN 978-0-312-38309-1
    1. Ruzak, Teddy (Fictitious character)—Fiction.   2. Private investigators—Fiction.   3. Knoxville (Tenn.)—Fiction.   I. Title.
    PS3625.A675H56 2010
    813'.6—dc22

                                                                      2009041536
                        First Edition: March 2010

                    10   9   8   7   6   5   4   3   2   1

To Sandy, mon chérie amour

ACT ONE

The Accused

SCENE ONE
The Office

A Sunny Morning in May

*T*his is not about sex," the woman said.

With my trusty mechanical pencil, I wrote "not about sex" beneath her name, "Katrina Bates."

"He's had many affairs, practically since day one of our marriage. On the second night of our honeymoon, he made a pass at our waitress."

I wrote, "Day one. Second night. Waitress." I stared at the words. Wouldn't that be day two?

"I was returning from the rest room and there it was: his hand rubbing her bottom."

"That's brazen," I said.

"He had an excuse," Katrina Bates said. She didn't elaborate. I wondered what plausible reason a groom could offer for placing his hand on a stranger's ass. I wrote, "Hand on bottom."

"Are you going to do that for the entire interview?" she asked. "Write down everything I say?"

"It helps to jog my memory."

"It was twenty years ago and has nothing to do with why I'm here, Mr. Ruzak."

"Well," I said. "Now I've written it, and if I erase it, a month from now I might forget what I erased and why I erased it and if I erased something that might be vitally important, and then I'd have to bug you about what it might have been, which you probably won't remember, either."

She blinked at me.

"So?"

"So now I'm stuck. I could draw a line through it," I offered.

"I don't care what you do with it. I was just asking why you think my husband's hand on that anonymous person's bottom twenty years ago could have anything to do with the reason I'm hiring you."

"That's a good question," I said. "Why are you hiring me?"

"I want you to find out if he's cheating on me."

I could have told her without so much as lifting a single investigative pinkie that the odds were pretty good that he was. Any guy who feels up the waitress on his honeymoon doesn't place fidelity high on his list. Still, I was a firm believer in the ability of people to change—even to change for the better.

"He's cheated on you before," I said.

"Many times," she said.

"This time you want proof."

"Yes."

"Because this time is different."

She nodded. Katrina Bates was an attractive woman. Middle-aged, with shoulder-length, chemically enhanced blond hair, moderately tall, blessed with good genes: prominent cheekbones, large, expressive blue eyes, and a long, graceful neck. And nice legs. With most women, the legs are usually the last to go.

"This time he denies it," I said.

"Vehemently."

"Hides it."

A nod. And a tear quivering in the corner of her right eye.

"Because this time it isn't meaningless," I went on. "This time it's love."

"You understand, Mr. Ruzak."

I wrote the word *love* on my legal yellow pad. She didn't protest. I slid the box of Kleenex toward her side of my desk. In my line of work, tissues were indispensable tools of the trade.

SCENE TWO
The Office

Two Weeks Later

*T*his isn't personal," the man said.

"I never said that," I said. "Never even thought it, Mr. Hinton."

"But the law is the law."

"Right. Because if it weren't, it wouldn't be."

"I have the injunction right here in my briefcase, but I don't need to show it to you, do I?"

"Oh, no need for that. You gave me a copy last time you were here. I have it tucked away somewhere, but you know organization was never my strong suit."

"No, that would be deceit and dishonesty."

"At least it's not redundancy," I said. Score one for Ruzak, but it was like a hitting a homer with empty bases, down by ten runs, with two outs in the bottom of the ninth. I folded my hands on the desktop and sat very still, holding myself carefully, like someone with a terminal illness. Hinton sat across from me, a little guy in a gray suit and bow tie—no kidding—who reminded me of Harry Truman, with the square head and round spectacles, the chin, square, but not quite so square as his head, thrust defiantly in my direction, as if he were daring me to pop it.

"I'm not a complete idiot, Mr. Ruzak," Hinton said, which I took as an implication that I was. "I know full well what you're up to."

"What?" I asked. "I complied with the court order. I shut the business down. We're not the Highly Effective Detection & Investigation Company anymore. Didn't you see the name on the door? The Research & Analysis Group, LLC."

"You can change the name on your door, but it doesn't change the fact that you are practicing private detection without a license, Mr. Ruzak."

"Well, we could quibble over semantics. What's your proof?"

"I don't have to prove anything. The burden is on you to prove otherwise."

"That seems downright un-American, Mr. Hinton. But wouldn't you agree it's awfully difficult to prove a negative? I can't prove I'm *not* doing something."

"Fair enough," he said. He had thin lips and they were drawn tight. Give 'em hell, Harry. "Your *company*"—sneered like a dirty word—"the Research & Analysis Group—what exactly does it do?"

"Conducts research."

"What kind of research?"

"The kind you analyze."

"Funny."

"People come to us with certain questions and we research them."

"What questions?"

"The kind that require research. I'm sorry, but I can't get into specifics."

"And why is that, Mr. Ruzak?"

"I can't really say, Mr. Hinton."

"Why?"

"I can't violate my clients' confidentiality."

"That applies to doctors and lawyers, Mr. Ruzak."

"And bankers. You forgot bankers."

"Is that it? Are you a banker?"

"No," I said patiently. "I'm a freelance researcher and analyst."

"'Analyst,'" he echoed. "What do you analyze?"

"The research."

"You may think this is humorous, Mr. Ruzak, but I assure you the judge will not."

"Probably not," I agreed. "You normally don't think of mirth as being a judicial quality."

"Never mind the specifics," he said. "In general, without divulging any names or particular circumstances, what is the nature of your research?"

"Well, in general, if you want to know specifically what I research, I would have to say those questions or issues that plague society in general."

"For example?"

"For example, say a client comes in wanting to know something about the past. I do that."

"Do what?"

"Research the past."

"By 'the past,' do you mean history? Are you a historian, Mr. Ruzak? Do you have clients who want to know a bit more about the Battle of Hastings?"

"That hasn't happened yet, but sure, if they wanted to know a bit more about the Battle of Hastings, I'd dig into it."

"My tenth grader has a report due next week on Napoléon. Perhaps you could help him."

"My rates are probably beyond the means of your average tenth grader, but I could give him a discount, based on our friendship," I said.

"Do you find it ironic, Mr. Ruzak, this frivolous mockery of justice even as you purport to pursue it?"

"Who said I purport to pursue justice?"

"You did when you said you solve problems that plague society in general."

"I didn't say I solved them. Nobody has, to my knowledge. I just add my light to the sum of light."

"I asked for an example."

"And I gave you one. The Battle of Hastings."

"*I* gave that example, Mr. Ruzak."

"Well, it doesn't matter to me who gets the credit."

"Are you stupid, Mr. Ruzak?"

"I'd hate to think so."

"Do you think I'm stupid?"

"I hardly know you."

"In order for you to practice private detection or research or analysis, or whatever the hell you want to call it, in the state of Tennessee, you must acquire a license from the Private Investigation and Polygraph Commission, of which I am a duly authorized representative. In order to acquire that license, you must meet certain criteria, including passing the official test, which you have failed to do *three times*, Mr. Ruzak. Now you can call yourself whatever you wish—researcher, analyst, consultant. . . . You can call yourself a hairstylist or hog butcher for all I care, but as long as you charge people to 'research' and 'analyze' their 'questions,' your activities fall under our jurisdiction and you are subject to substantial penalties and fines for doing so without obtaining a license to practice the same."

"I'm not a detective," I said firmly.

"I'll get the proof, Mr. Ruzak," he promised. He stood up. "And then I'll be back with a warrant for your arrest."

"An arrest warrant? For what?"

"For contempt of court, Mr. Ruzak." He placed his round hat upon his square head—wasn't Truman a haberdasher?—and strode from my office in his perfectly shined shoes with a slight squeak in the left heel.

The outer door slammed and Felicia came in, slid into the chair Hinton had just vacated, and we regarded each other for a moment. I looked away first. I was her boss and technically the top dog in our little operation, but from the get-go Felicia had this way of making me feel too big for whatever space we happened to occupy, even outdoor spaces, and the smaller the space, the more intense the sensation. In the car with her, I felt as big as a Macy's parade balloon. But to be a little more precise, it was more like the space around me shrank than I expanded to fill it. Pretty women usually had that effect on me. So did furniture salesmen, and that was hard to decipher.

"I told you it was a bad idea," I said, meaning scraping the old name off the door and slapping on a new one. "This Hinton guy is relentless."

"It wouldn't have been necessary in the first place if you had passed the exam," she replied.

"What do you think it was?" I asked. Then I answered my own question. "The Yellow Pages. We're still listed under private investigators."

"Does it matter?"

"We have a couple options," I began. "Close up shop and hope with the test that the fourth time is the charm, or keep the doors open and the devil take the hindmost."

"The devil take the what?"

"Maybe I could pay somebody to take the test for me. It's coming up next month."

"How you've changed since you took up private law enforcement."

"Einstein flunked out of school."

"Is that something you know, something you think you remember, or something you're making up out of whole cloth to justify your failures?"

"He may have dropped out."

"Maybe that's it: You went into the wrong field. Try physics next; you've so much in common with Einstein."

"'Genius is close to madness,'" I said.

"There is an element of that," she said. "The second part."

"I took the wrong tack," I said. "I should have come clean and begged for mercy. All self-respecting sadists and bureaucrats suck on that teat."

"'Suck on that . . . teat'?"

"Better to sin and ask for forgiveness later."

"That's your fallback position, isn't it, Ruzak? Quoting aphorisms, like it accomplishes something."

"The ironic thing is," I called after her as she headed for the door, "I actually believe I'm helping people, and the state is going to arrest me for it."

Of course the truth was that the state was going to arrest me for an entirely different transgression, but since reading somewhere that we lived in a postironic age, I had taken on a personal mission to keep irony alive, at least within my minuscule sphere. Teddy Ruzak: researcher, analyst, master ironist.

Felicia appeared in the doorway, Gucci knockoff over her shoulder, hand on hip, one leg crossed over the other, and, it being spring, there was a lot of bare leg to be crossed. Felicia had well-developed calves from her years as a waitress at the Old City Diner. She also possessed a pair of the finest knees I had ever seen, not that I spent a lot of time studying women's knees, but there it was. She wore no panty hose. Nobody wore panty hose anymore. I only knew this because one day I asked her why she didn't wear panty hose and she informed me that nobody wore them anymore.

"I'm leaving," she said.

"It's only two o'clock."

"I have to pick up Tommy from preschool."

"Bringing him back here?" I liked the kid and everything, but he was a little wild and tended to crawl into my lap and play with my letter opener.

"Can't," she said. "Gotta run some errands. Let me know if you get arrested. I'd hate to get up tomorrow for nothing."

She turned, and I would like to say my gaze did not fall upon her backside on her way out.

I shut down her computer, turned off the reception room lights, filled up the mister in the john just off my office, and watered the row of ferns on the window ledge behind my desk. Then, because I couldn't think of doing anything else that wasn't an obvious waste of time or an embarrassingly obvious bit of procrastination (reminding me of a funny T-shirt I had seen recently that said PROCRASTINA-TOR'S TO-DO LIST: I . . .), I pulled the Bates file from *B* section of the cabinet—not hard to find, since it was the *only* file in the *B* section— and dialed the cell number Katrina Bates had provided.

He picked up on the third ring.

"This is Tom."

"Tom," I said. "You don't know me, but I'm a friend of Katrina."

A beat, then: "Okay. . . ." He was waiting for the punch line.

"She doesn't know I'm calling," I said. "And she probably wouldn't be too happy with the fact that I am. But I didn't say I wouldn't and she never said I couldn't."

Another beat. I dug his picture out of the file. Lean, with dark eyes and thin lips. A pale complexion set off nicely by a full flowing mane of hair slightly darker than his eyes, going gray at the temples, but a steel gray, a battleship gray, which gave his youthful face a bit of gravitas. There was something vampirish about him. The dark looks and what he was wearing, too: a tuxedo. He was clutching some kind of trophy or award. He wasn't smiling. He stood ramrod-straight, head tilted back, chin up, looking down his long, aristocratic nose at the camera; he reminded me of a Victorian gentleman at the turn of the last century, when the sun never set on the empire, not merely sure but cocksure of his just deserts. *That's right; I'm the dude with the trophy, not you, and not this fat guy with the triple chin next to me. Me.*

"Who are you?" he asked.

"A friend of Katrina," I replied. "You don't know me."

"I know all her friends." *Ergo, you cannot be someone I do not know.* Tom Bates taught mathematics at the university. He had published twelve books and held about the same number of degrees, a couple being from Harvard, with a smattering of others from places like MIT and Boston University. In college, he played polo. Polo! He spoke seven languages. He sat on the boards of half a dozen foundations. He was a personal friend of Bill Gates and Steve Jobs. Now that's balance; that's covering all your bases. In

his spare time, he liked to play chess or one of the five musical in-
struments he had mastered since the age of five. He also liked to
paint; one of his paintings hung in the Museum of Modern Art.
Fortunately for poor Tom, what he lacked in the brains and talent
departments, he more than made up for in wealth. Tom Bates was
rich. Not Bill Gates rich, more like Donald Trump rich, except
his money was old, extremely old, going back to the founding of
the republic. Katrina had lowered her voice as she confessed this
one dark stain upon the Bates family name, the shadow cast from
the distant past. The acorn seed of their affluence was fertilized
by the blood of human chattel: Tom's ancestors had made their
dough in the slave trade. After that practice was outlawed, they
took the money and invested it in other, less odious ventures—
textiles, manufacturing, real estate. The Bates family, according to Katrina, owned half the state of Massachusetts. "All the
Bates men were geniuses," she told me. "Geniuses at making
money. Except Tom. It's the one thing he's terrible at. He's a fi-
nancial retard. Maybe it was some kind of genetic mutation, but
his genius doesn't touch money." It gave me some sick satisfaction
when she said that. Up to that point, I'd been feeling pretty bad
about myself vis-à-vis Mr. Tom Bates and his good looks, his
twelve books, his degrees, his painting hanging in MoMA, his
virtuosity at the violin and cello. Not that I was any better at
making a buck, but it proved that in at least one area we were
equal or near-equal retards.

"Well," I said. "You don't know me. Look, I'll get right to it.
She knows."

"Knows . . ."

"She doesn't have proof, not yet, but she's pretty intent on getting some, and you probably don't want her to see the kind of
proof she wants to see."

He's so quiet at first, I thought we'd been cut off. I said hello. He said, "Yes." That was it. Just "yes."

"So I was thinking that maybe for the good of everybody involved, you should do the manly thing and fess up, break it off, and devote yourself to a—what's the best way to put this?—a more monogamous lifestyle."

He said, "Who the hell is this? Who are you?"

"A friend of Katrina," I said for the third time.

The line went dead. I didn't call back. He hadn't given me the opportunity to tell him what kind of proof his wife wanted. It wasn't the kind I was eager to obtain, hence the call to urge him to confess and relieve me of the obligation.

SCENE THREE
The Sterchi Building

A Few Hours Later

The man named Whittaker was lurking in the lobby. I stepped inside the vestibule and he slipped inside my personal space.

"Mr. Ruzak," he said. "You know who I am."

"You bet," I said. "You're the assistant manager."

"Manager now."

"Well. Congratulations on the promotion."

He trailed me to the elevator.

"Mr. Ruzak, we've received more reports of you walking a dog on the grounds."

"'Reports'?"

"From residents."

The elevator doors slid open. We stepped inside. I deduced he was coming with me, based on the fact that he now stood beside me in the elevator that was rising toward my floor.

"The Sterchi is now and has always been a pet-free facility," Whittaker said.

"I know," I said. "Every time I see you, you tell me that."

The doors opened. I stepped into the hall. He followed. He was standing so close, I could smell his cologne.

"The lease is unequivocal on that point. I have a copy of it right here, if you'd like to review it."

"I have my own copy," I said. "Which I review every night. Thanks anyway."

"Then you're familiar with the provision under Paragraph F, Section Five."

I gave it my best shot. "Right. No pets allowed."

He trailed me a couple steps back as I made for my door.

"Actually, that provision guarantees management's right of ingress."

"'Right of ingress'?"

"We may enter your apartment at any time for just cause."

"You've gone in my apartment?"

We were now standing at the ingress point, my door. I felt my face growing hot in response to this violation—not mine, his.

"Keeping an animal in this building is grounds for nullification of your lease and, ultimately, eviction," Whittaker said.

"Of me or the alleged pet?"

"Mr. Ruzak, we could parse words here, but you see what I'm getting at."

"Well, I certainly can tell where you've been."

He reached into his briefcase. I flinched. "You're about to hand me a formal eviction notice," I said.

He pulled out a single sheet of paper with the Sterchi Management Company's letterhead.

"Thirty days' notice, Mr. Ruzak. The dog . . . or you. Have a great evening."

"He's completely housebroken," I said, following him back to the elevator. "And he never barks. He's never so much as whined. If he were human, he'd be one of those monks, the kind who takes the vow of silence."

"Thirty days, Mr. Ruzak," Whittaker repeated. He stepped into the car. I remained in the hall. The doors closed upon his triumphant smile.

Archie was sitting up in his crate, mouth open slightly; I could see the tip of his tongue. Ours wasn't exactly a joyous reunion, but it never was. Archie stepped out, I stepped back, and we stared at each other across a space as vast as the universe. Archie was a beagle mix, with the classic beagle markings of white and brown and the thin tail that arched gracefully over his back. That tail never moved unless the door buzzer rang or he heard footsteps in the hall, and then it all but vanished in a frenzied blur as he rushed the door. Inevitably, the bell fell silent, the footfalls faded, and Archie would collapse against the door and lift those soulful eyes up to mine with an attitude of such disappointment and loss that it never failed to bring me to tears, and not entirely empathetic tears, either.

"This isn't another way station like the pound," I would tell him. "This is home."

I don't think he ever quite bought it, though. Sterchi Management certainly did not. Animals have a sixth sense about natural disasters; maybe that extended to personal ones, as well. A couple of years back, I watched a TV special about this dog who smelled the cancer growing inside his master's lungs. I wondered if Archie had "heard" the bell tolling upon Whittaker's or one of his lackeys' trespass into his territory, had somehow seen the handwriting on the wall.

"It's okay," I told him as he sat staring at the front door, his back turned toward me. "If push comes to shove, I'll move."

He ignored me. I was used to it.

When you live alone, you rely on ritual. Walk the dog, check your messages, separate the mail (bills, junk, catalogs), change out of your work clothes, cook dinner, load the dishwasher, sprawl on the sofa and channel-surf for a couple of hours, surf the Net, watch a video of a drunk girl singing on YouTube, walk the dog again, check your messages again on the slim chance someone called while you were walking the dog, wash up for bed, lie in bed for an hour and chase sleep. The only variation that night was I didn't have to sneak Archie down the stairs and out the back door, since Whittaker knew of his existence. My mother had a favorite saying: "There's nothing done in the dark that doesn't eventually come out in the light." She used that one on me all the time, especially when I was a teenager. Her way of warning me against the evils of alcohol, drugs, and unprotected sex. Particularly the sex: I had a girlfriend my senior year, Tiffany, who dumped me after I flunked out of the Police Academy—for a guy named Bill Hill, a name I was doomed always to remember. As far as I knew, she still lived in Knoxville, but I never saw her after she dumped me and married Bill. In my fantasies, I'd run into her at the grocery store or gas station, and she'd say, "So what are you up to now, Teddy?" and I'd say, "Oh, I have my own detective agency now, with an office downtown," or something like that, and somehow I'd be able to work in the fact that my secretary was a dead ringer for Lauren Bacall, from the long, shapely legs to the luxurious fall of blond hair, even possessing the same throaty quality when she talked. In my fantasy, Tiffany had four children, all under the age of six, had gained twenty-five pounds, and was living on food stamps because Bill Hill had a drinking problem or maybe was in prison or even had left her for a woman who was not twenty-five pounds overweight and did not have four children, all under the age of six. It was a difficult fantasy to resist, but I tried to; it bordered on cruelty toward a girl whom I'd honestly thought I loved.

My cell phone rang a little after ten, between the brushing of teeth and the slow march toward sleep. I didn't recognized the number and debated whether to answer. I got a lot of wrong numbers, usually for a fellow named Jackson, whose number must have been one digit different from mine. I was irrationally jealous of Jackson: He got many more calls than I did.

"Mr. Ruzak," the woman on the other end said, with an emphasis on the first word: "*Mr.* Ruzak."

"That's me," I said. "Who're you?"

"This is Katrina Bates."

"Oh. Hey. I was gonna call you."

"Is that what happened? You dialed the wrong number by mistake?"

"The odds favor that," I said, deciding to fake it, since I had no idea what she was getting at. "I hardly ever dial one on purpose."

"I didn't hire you to *confront* him about infidelity; I hired you to *confirm* the infidelity."

"He told you."

"Mr. Ruzak, I don't pretend to know your business. If I knew your business, I wouldn't have hired you; I would have done it myself. But it seems to me the last thing you'd want to do is contact your target and let them know the jig is up."

"That seems reasonable," I said. "But, you know, detective work is a lot like plumbing. Sometimes you gotta attack the clog head-on."

"But now he knows I know, he knows you know, and won't that make catching him that much harder, if not impossible?"

"He may know I know, but he doesn't know who I am or what I look like. Anyway, who I am or what I look like isn't the point. The point is, these things are best solved by the parties directly involved."

"So . . . what does that mean, Mr. Ruzak? I didn't hire you to fix my marriage. If I wanted someone to fix my marriage, don't you think I would have hired a marriage counselor?"

"My secretary keeps trying to get me to see someone," I confessed. "She's convinced I have issues."

"What?"

"Abandonment issues. My dad was never around very much when I was growing up; then he died when I was pretty young, and then my mom died. After that. After I grew up. So now I have some problems with intimacy. The difficulty I have with that— with seeing someone, I mean—is I've always been a by-your-bootstraps sort of guy. You know, tying yourself to the mainmast and riding out the storm."

There was a pause.

"Mr. Ruzak, are you drunk?"

"No."

"So this is how you normally talk?"

"I know," I said. "It's always been a problem of mine, kind of exacerbated by years of working the graveyard shift. There's a monologist flavor to it."

"You don't seem to understand why I called. I'm upset with you. I paid you a five-hundred-dollar retainer and you pick up the phone and tell my husband I know he's having an affair!"

"What did he say?" I asked. "Did he confess?"

"Of course he didn't confess!"

"Well, I thought it was worth a shot."

"I don't want a confession. I couldn't care less whether he comes clean. And I don't want to waste any more time or money trying to fix something that's irretrievably broken."

"Then I'm confused."

"Obviously!"

"If you don't love him, why do you care?"

"This isn't about love, you idiot." By this point, she had lost it. "Didn't I say that when I hired you?"

"No. You said it isn't about sex." Good thing I had made a note about that.

"Well, it isn't," she sobbed. "It isn't about either."

"Then what's it about?"

"Revenge."

"Oh. Well, I'm not sure I want to be in the revenge business."

"What? What does that mean? Are you dropping my case?"

"I'll tell you why I called him, Mrs. Bates. I called him because honesty is better than deceit. That's one of the core principles I subscribe to; otherwise, I'd be in a entirely different line of work, the kind you can get arrested for, though there's a strong possibility I'm going to be arrested for my current line, which is what you might call irony. Call it hokey and naïve, but I see my job as showing the person to the door; it's totally up to them whether they walk through it or not."

"Door? What door? What the hell are you talking about, Mr. Ruzak?"

"The door that opens to the truth, the thing that sets you free, the passage from darkness into light. You know."

"Your secretary's right. You *do* need help."

"You're firing me," I said, and not without a drop of desire.

"Maybe I've seen too many movies, watched too many TV shows about detectives."

"Most people have. And not just about detectives."

"Because this is not what I expected. This isn't what I expected at all."

"Did you tell him I was?"

"Was what?"

"A detective."

"Of course not!"

"If you had, do you think he would have come clean?"

"I know what you're trying to do. You're trying to make a point about *my* integrity. You think I should have told him who you were."

"Like I said," I said. "I'm not the point."

"Well, that's certainly not true now! You've *made* yourself the point, Mr. Ruzak; you picked up the phone and told him I know he's having an affair!"

I finally got it. "He pulled a switcheroo."

"Excuse me? 'Switcheroo'?"

"He changes the issue from him to me. He denied the affair, taking that issue off the table, and made me the issue. 'I know all her friends,' he said to me, so he says to you, 'Who is this guy calling me claiming to be one?' He's turned it from his secret to your secret. That's pretty damn smart."

"And you're surprised?"

"Impressed."

"Well, I'm not." She didn't say, but I suspected it wasn't Tom she wasn't impressed with. "He's going to be very careful now. Much more careful than before, making your job all the more difficult. He might even break it off."

"That would be a bad thing?"

She muttered something I couldn't make out. It might have been "I did it" or the word *idiot*. Given the context, the latter made more sense.

"Mrs. Bates," I said. "I'm getting a little confused."

"Oh, *really*?"

"You hired me to uncover this affair you suspect him of having, but tell me it isn't about sex and it isn't about love. Why do you need proof? Why don't you just divorce him?"

"I told you why."

"When?"

"Just now!"

"Oh, right. Revenge. But what revenge? Don't most spouses in your position exact revenge by . . . Well, I don't know of a delicate way to put this. . . ."

"Oh, don't think I haven't thought about it. Don't think I haven't had rich fantasies of putting a bullet into his Ivy League brain."

I was a little shocked by that. "I was thinking more along the lines of you dipping into the same well."

"Cheating on him? I could never cheat on Tom. I love him. He's the love of my life."

I rubbed my temple. This was getting bad. Maybe my problem was one of acuity, or the lack thereof, and had nothing to do with fear of intimacy. Maybe I just didn't get it. I wondered if that was why detective work had appealed to me from an early age. Maybe it wasn't solving crimes I was after, but solving mysteries, as in the ineffable kind. Like women.

I said, nearing exhaustion, "I thought you said it wasn't about love."

"If I didn't care, I wouldn't want to destroy him."

"But I thought that whole deal was about forgiveness," I said.

"What deal?"

"Love."

She gave a bitter little laugh. "You obviously have never been in love."

"Well, I'm not sure that's true," I said. "You really shouldn't assume that, Mrs. Bates. But it is funny you brought it up, because I was thinking about this girl I was engaged to a few years back; just today I was thinking about her and kind of fantasizing how things might be with her now, and they weren't what you might call pleasant. They were downright grim. So I do get your point."

"What happened?" she asked. "Did she dump you?"

"For a guy named Bill Hill. I didn't know him very well, but his prospects were better, at least at the time; he was making a pretty good living and I had just been kicked out of the Police Academy. I understood why she did it, but understanding the bitter pill rarely makes swallowing it easier. Also there was the fact that Bill's living was sales. That was also my father's living, when he was living, and that might have raised some Oedipal issues."

"I just don't want to hurt anymore," she said. "I've been hurting for so long. I just want the hurt to go away."

"And you think destroying your husband is going to do that?"

"I've tried practically everything else."

Then Katrina Bates did a startling thing: She asked to meet me for a drink. I told her I was in my pajamas. She laughed, for some reason.

"It never dies, does it, Mr. Ruzak?"

"What?"

"Hope. Deep in my heart, I don't really want to destroy him. Deep in my heart, I'm hoping when I confront him with the proof, he'll come back to me. I suppose that's pretty naïve."

"No," I said. "Human."

SCENE FOUR
The Whittle Building

The Next Day

Springtime in Knoxville stinks, at least if you're within ten feet of a blooming Bradford pear tree. The delicate white blossoms, thousands per tree, floated against the backdrop of dark boughs and bright green leaves in a kind of mockery of winter, emitting a stench on a stomach-churning scale somewhere between BO and rotting flesh. I had a theory that the evolutionary purpose was to drive away predatory insects. The smell didn't seem to bother the bees; they danced from bloom to bloom in a highly coordinated waltz, never so much as brushing another's wing tip. Humans are often clumsy, but nature on its surface never seems to be. Of course, that was nineteenth-century thinking, which put me a good two hundred years behind the times, but I was a romantic at heart. The alternative was just so damned depressing.

Felicia and I ducked our heads beneath the noxious blooms that hung above the sidewalk on Main Street. Later in the month, the walkway would be slick with fallen, rotting petals. We were on our way to lunch at the cafeteria in the federal building on the corner of Main and Gay Street, where on Tuesdays the special was roast beef and gravy.

I held my breath until we cleared the canopy, and the sunlight felt like a warm hand on the back of my neck.

"I'm not sure you're being entirely honest with yourself, Ruzak," Felicia said. She leaned slightly toward me as she talked, which put the top of her head about three inches from my nose. I smelled peaches.

"About what?" I asked.

"Maybe you didn't call Tom Bates to show him truth's door. Maybe you called him to avoid having to catch him in the act."

"Meaning I'm not as noble as I think I am?"

"Meaning you're not so different from everyone else."

"Lazy?"

"Expert rationalizer."

"Maybe I'm just a romantic."

"You considered that a likely outcome? He comes home, confesses everything, then falls to his knees and begs for forgiveness?"

"He's got a lot to lose."

"And you call yourself a romantic."

I put a hand on her elbow as we jaywalked across Main. The entrance to the complex was in the middle of the block.

"It's not a quality you usually find in a gumshoe," I admitted. "Though it always held this medieval kind of appeal for me. You know, the knight in shining armor, the chivalric code and all that."

"Well, Sir Theodore," she said, "I guess I know who's buying lunch."

"I always buy lunch," I said.

She pulled from my grasp when we reached the opposite sidewalk.

The Howard Baker Jr. Federal Building hadn't always been a

federal building. It had been built by a man named Whittle, who named it after himself, the Whittle Building. Old-timers still called it that. Whittle had gone broke and sold it to the government, which of course was broke, too, but that didn't matter; it was the government.

We carried our trays out of the crowded cafeteria to dine al fresco in the center courtyard, were small metal tables were placed strategically in the shade on the north side of the building, far from the pungent pear trees that grew in the middle. Felicia drizzled a quarter-size dab of balsamic vinaigrette onto her salad. Felicia always took her dressing on the side. She spread its webby looking tendrils across the shards of Boston lettuce with the tines of her plastic fork.

"So maybe I was a little uncomfortable with the role," I said. "You know, the instrument of another man's destruction."

"Ruzak, that instrument is located inside Tom Bates's pants."

"And I had no idea until last night that the goal even was destruction."

"What the hell did you think it was?"

I shrugged. Was I just a naïve, immature human being, deficient in those life experiences that make us cynical and world-weary? Or was it a congenital defect, a flaw in my character that doomed me to a lifetime of ingenuousness? And which would be worse?

"I should drop this case," I said. "Should I drop this case? Say I get the proof and she uses it to destroy him professionally and personally. What does that make me?"

"How many executives of Smith & Wesson go on trial for murder, Ruzak?"

"Maybe that's the wrong analogy. Maybe it's more like the tobacco companies. Anyway, like I said before, I like the knight-in-shining-armor metaphor better than the hired gun one."

"Well then, you should drop it."

"Should I?"

"People with a lot to lose do desperate things, Teddy. And now he knows, thanks to you, that she suspects something and that there's some stranger out there asking questions. What if he catches you attempting to catch him?"

It struck me she was worried about me.

"Careful is my middle name," I said.

She smiled, and the center of her nose crinkled.

"What *is* your middle name? I never knew."

"Alan."

"Theodore Alan Ruzak. T.A.R."

"Why is that funny?"

At the table next to us, an elderly man was sitting with a woman at least half his age. Probably one of the judges with his clerk or secretary. He was handsome in a distinguished kind of way; she was mousy, with a pinched face; and I was irrationally proud: My secretary was prettier than his secretary.

"Still, if you decide to keep on it, take your gun," Felicia advised. "You never know."

"He's an egghead," I said. "Ostrich-sized. A mathematics professor at UT."

"Lemme guess. The other woman is a student."

I nodded. "That's what Katrina suspects. One of his."

"Naughty."

"You would think somebody that smart would have a little more self-control."

"Love makes us stupid, Ruzak."

"Well," I said. "There goes that excuse. I don't know why, but after she chewed me out last night, she asked me out for drinks."

"She hit on you?"

"It was weird."

"Maybe not. She's what, pushing forty-five? Plus, her husband's screwing around with a twenty-something coed."

"She didn't strike me as insecure."

"Okay. Maybe she just found you incredibly hot."

"You're kidding. That's okay."

"Seriously, though, you find her attractive."

I stirred my pile of green beans. The cafeteria cooked them with bacon. Roast beef, gravy, white bread, and bacon. What was I doing to myself? My adoration of fat and carbs overrode my basic survival instinct. *Love makes us stupid.*

"For some reason, ever since she hired me, I've been thinking about my old girlfriend Tiffany. Did I ever tell you about her?"

"She dumped you for a guy named Bill."

"Bill Hill," I said. "He was a salesman, like my dad. Do you think I remember his name because it rhymes or because he was a salesman like my dad?"

"Why are you changing the subject, Ruzak? You find Katrina Bates attractive. It's okay to say yes, you know."

"I'm a professional, Felicia," I said. "And the first rule is never get personally involved with your clients."

"You wanna know how I met Bob?" Bob was Felicia's boyfriend. "My old boss at the diner made all of us take a CPR class, in case a customer had a coronary trying to eat the slop he passed off as food. Bob taught the class. I took one look at him giving that dummy mouth-to-mouth, and that was it for me."

"Well, your old boss was technically the client in that scenario," I said. The image of Felicia's boyfriend sucking on the face of a blow-up doll disturbed me in a way that it obviously hadn't Felicia.

"You always miss the point, Ruzak. She won't always be your client."

"Why are you pushing Katrina Bates on me?"

"I worry about you."

"Why?"

"Because being alone is no damn good."

"I have Archie." Though maybe not for long. I told her about Whittaker and the thirty-day letter.

"Looks like you're moving."

"That's one option."

"You're thinking of getting rid of him?"

"We can't seem to bond. You know, I've had that dog for what, five months now, and there's absolutely no sense of connection. He avoids me. I open his crate and he drags himself out with this look like 'Oh, there *he* is again,' like maybe he was hoping somebody different would show up. So I've been buying him all these treats, chewies and bones and dried pigs' ears, coming home every night like a rejected suitor with another gift, another bauble to induce his affection, and nothing works. He finds the spot farthest away from me, drops the goody between his paws, doesn't touch it, just stares at me, while I'm slowly going broke trying to buy his love. It's psychologically devastating, Felicia. Dogs don't normally behave this way, or they wouldn't be dogs. Dogs are easy. Dogs are whores when it comes to affection. You know it's bad when you can't even buy a dog's love."

"You could be looking at it from the wrong angle," she said.

"Well, it wouldn't be the first time."

"It could be the dog and not you. Maybe that's why he ended up in the pound in the first place."

"I'd rather find a good home for him before doing that."

"I told you, Ruzak," she said, knowing exactly where this was leading. "Bob's allergic."

"I guess I could put an ad in the paper."

"This dog is the least of your worries," she said.

"Or find someone like that guy on TV who speaks their language. You know they have animal shrinks now? Maybe Archie is bipolar or depressed or suffering from post-traumatic stress. Maybe it's not a pig's ear he needs, but a pill. I took him to the vet, you know, to rule out any physical cause, and he checked out fine. She suggested I spend more time with him, take him to the office with me, outings at the doggy park, long car rides through the countryside, maybe a picnic by a mountain stream."

"She wants you to date your dog?"

"Maybe I should borrow someone else's dog and take it home. Love it up all night to make him jealous."

"This conversation is getting very weird," Felicia said. "You're going to stage a one-night stand with another dog to make your dog jealous?"

"But that wouldn't solve my Whittaker problem."

"No, that would be a reflection of something much more disturbing."

"Ruzak's so unlovable, even a dog won't have him?"

"It might not be entirely altruistic," she said, tiptoeing.

"Because even love has an agenda?"

"Especially love," she said.

SCENE FIVE
Knoxville Riverwalk

Ten Days Later

We bought Italian ices from a Hispanic vendor—lemon for me, cherry for her—and strolled along the promenade, between the steep hill cutting off the view of downtown and the murky waters of the Tennessee River, above us the sky cloudless and brilliant blue after an early-morning spring shower that had polished the new leaves to that particularly aggressive tone of bright green and left the dirt that was yet untouched by concrete, our busy human touch, as moist and pliant as a young girl's skin. "What's your dog's name?" asked Katrina Bates, watching Archie strain at the leash. Despite hours of practice and having all the proper techniques fully memorized, I still hadn't been able to get this dog to heel. A thirty-minute walk always made me feel like the victim of some kind of medieval torture.

"Archie."

"He doesn't look like an Archie to me."

"I didn't name him."

"You could rename him."

"I would, but he's got enough problems."

I pulled him off the hill and edged closer to the water. He froze; a mother duck and her brood paddling in the slight chop a dozen yards out had caught his eye. I took advantage of the break and shoveled a couple of spoonfuls of flavored ice into my mouth.

"I never come down here," she said. "It's nice."

"That's Baptist Hospital over there," I said, pointing to the bluff across the river, upon which the hospital brooded. "Where my mother died."

"Recently?"

"It's all relative," I replied.

"You were close to your mom."

"I take her fresh flowers every week. Stand there and talk to her headstone."

"It must make you feel better."

"And worse. I mean, wouldn't it have meant more if I'd taken her flowers every week when she was alive? I didn't. It isn't for the dead, all this ritual; it's for us."

"Isn't everything?"

We sat on a bench to finish our treats. Once he'd thoroughly vetted the area with his busy nose, Archie planted himself beside Katrina and laid his head on her thigh. I pulled on his leash. She said it was okay, that she didn't mind, and scratched him gently just above his eyes, which were turned soulfully upon her face.

"What a sweet dog," she said.

"You bet," I said, albeit with a sour taste in my mouth, and it wasn't from the lemon.

"They say dogs take on the personalities of their owners," she said.

"Well, he's always been kind of aloof . . . at least with me."

"Is that what you meant by 'problems'?"

"Right. The problem could be from my end."

"I've heard dogs prefer one gender over another. Some dogs like women; some like men."

"Well, he likes you."

"Tom's dog hates me. He urinates on my clothes."

"Could be a territorial response."

"It usually is when it comes to males."

"I meant not personal."

"I know what you meant," she said, with a slight emphasis on the word *you*. She looked up from Archie to me. Or I assumed she was looking at me. Her face was turned toward me, but her eyes were hidden behind oversized Chanel sunglasses.

"What have you found out?" she asked.

"I still don't have any proof, if that's what you're asking."

"Then why did you want to see me?"

"I've been following her for almost two weeks now. Apartment to class to work to bar to gym to a concert in Market Square, then back to the apartment, and not a single Tom sighting. Not one."

"You've been following . . . who?"

"Kinsey Brock. The girl. Woman. The other woman. She is the one, right?"

"Right. But why were you following her?"

"To catch her with Tom."

"No, why were you following *her*? Why weren't you following Tom?"

"Oh, I wouldn't follow Tom."

"Why wouldn't you follow Tom?"

"Because Tom knows me. Or knows *about* me."

"How could he possibly know that?"

"I called him," I reminded her.

"So?"

"So he knows you're onto him and knows you've told somebody and he's going to be hypervigilant."

"Funny, that's what I thought I hired you to be."

"Plus, I didn't think either one of them would ever suspect I'd follow her."

"I certainly wouldn't. Isn't it possible that your call would make *both* of them hypervigilant? And the fact that you didn't catch them together might be proof of *that* and not the other?"

"Proof of what?"

"Of their hypervigilance."

"I'm just in the data-gathering phase of the investigation," I said. "Research, then analysis." That sounded condescending, so to soften it, I added, "It'll be okay," which sounded even more condescending, so I added, "You gotta have faith."

"Faith in what? In men?"

"In the future. That everything will turn out okay. Like the world's running out of gas, but gas was never good for the world to begin with. Plus, we're pretty smart, as species go, a lot smarter than the dinosaurs were, and maybe if an asteroid doesn't hit us, we'll figure our way out of this mess."

"Gas . . . dinosaurs? I'm confused, Mr. Ruzak."

"Me, too," I said. "It's a little overwhelming when you think about it. But you can't be afraid of change."

"What's any of that have to do with my husband dipping his wick in a coed?"

"Not much," I admitted. "Probably nothing at all. I have this tendency to go off on philosophical tangents." I was somewhat taken aback. Katrina Bates was an upper-class, well-educated woman, a graduate of Dartmouth, she told me, and here she was saying something like "dipping his wick."

"It doesn't strike me as being limited to philosophy," she said.

"Here's my point—"

"Oh, *good.*"

"Maybe I haven't proved they aren't, but it raises a legitimate question about the major premise that they are. Are you sure he's dip—uh, seeing her? Maybe I'm following the wrong person."

"It's her," she said firmly.

"How do you know?"

"How I know is my business, Mr. Ruzak."

"Mine, too," I said, meaning it wasn't entirely my fault I might have spent ten days following the wrong person. "You did hire me, Mrs. Bates."

"Katrina," she said.

"Right," I said. "Katrina. And I don't pretend to know much about torrid affairs, seeing I've never actually been involved in one, but isn't the inability to keep your hands off each other one of their chief characteristics?"

"I'm not going to argue with you, Mr. Ruzak."

I sighed. So many arguments begin with that. "Teddy," I said, acquiescing.

"Yes. Teddy. The issue is that since I hired you, you've alerted the target his secret is no longer secret and wasted your time spying on the wrong person, neither of which accomplished the thing I'm paying you to do. It's enough to make me question my decision to hire you."

"Well, say I have this mysterious rattle in my car. I take it to the mechanic and he charges me five hundred bucks to fix it. Then after a few dozen miles, the rattle comes back. Do I take it back to the same shop? Give him a second chance or demand my money back? Or do I find another mechanic with a more thorough knowledge of the whys and wherefores of car rattles?"

"To be perfectly honest, you wouldn't have been my first choice," she said, turning her face away. Archie lifted his head off her lap to follow her gaze across the river. She scratched behind his floppy ears. It struck me a stranger might think he belonged to her. "I would have preferred that other agency."

"The Velman Group," I said. An easy guess: The Velman Group was the only big detective outfit in town.

She nodded, absently pulling on one of Archie's ears. "But I couldn't go there," she said.

"Why?" I asked. And then I got it. "A conflict of interest?"

She nodded again. "Tom hired them about six years ago."

"To follow you?"

"He was certain I was having an affair. I wasn't. But I was afraid if I went there, they might tell him."

"So you hired me."

"And *you* told him." Her laughter was soft and bitter. "He's very smart and very talented and he's had every advantage in life. He has looks and money, brains, ability, and privilege, but none of that, *none* of it, is worth a tinker's damn without luck. You have to be lucky, and he is. And you're a perfect example of it, Teddy."

She stood. Archie stood with her, his tail swinging as he looked up at her face with what I swore was caninc adoration.

I couldn't see her eyes behind the designer shades, just my reflection in them, a big guy with a slightly crooked nose and in need of a haircut. My focus shifted to her lips, the bottom one slightly plumper and redder than the top, stained from the Italian ice, I guessed. Her makeup was otherwise flawless, not overly applied; I wondered if she used that new mineral foundation that was all the rage, or that I assumed was all the rage, based solely on the commercials, which ran endlessly on late-night TV. My original assessment of her had been a little off the mark: She wasn't a pretty woman; she was a beautiful woman. Beautiful—and very, very angry.

"You're fired," she said.

SCENE SIX
The Office

Two Days Later

The man in the gray suit showed up while I was messing with my new camcorder, trying to figure out which button ejected the mini-DVD. Like a lot of guys, I refused to waste my time reading the instructions; I preferred to waste it fooling with the gadget. The same principle applied to my aversion to self-help books.

Felicia showed him in, and I couldn't help but notice the certain lightness in her step as she sashayed out of the room.

He was impeccably groomed; his hair shone with product; and there was something George Clooneyish about his looks, especially around the eyes. He led with his prominent chin, thrusting it toward me as he leaned over the desk to shake my hand.

"Teddy Ruzak! It's a pleasure."

He pressed a business card into my hand and plopped himself down in the visitor's chair, tugging on his jacket so it didn't bunch up around his shoulders. Then he adjusted the crease in his slacks. I looked at the card. *Dresden Falks/The Velman Group, LLC/Investigations & Security.*

"I was in the neighborhood and thought I'd make a courtesy

call," Dresden Falks said. "Though the name on the door threw me a little. Thought you were the DIC."

"We changed the name," I said.

"Why?"

"To avoid confusion."

"What kind of confusion?"

"The legal kind."

"There's always plenty of that to go around," Falks said. He smiled forcefully at me, the same aggressive smile you find at fundamentalist churches and used-car lots. His teeth appeared to be veneered. "You know what we call that down at Velman? 'Job security.'"

He laughed like he had gotten off a good joke. The door opened and Felicia pranced back into the room with an Evian and a cocktail napkin. Where the hell had she gotten a cocktail napkin? She set the bottle down in front of him and asked him if she could get him anything else. He told her he was all set and then made a show of turning in his chair to watch the gluteal muscles bunch beneath her skirt upon her slower-than-usual exit. I thought of airplanes, for some reason, and the fact that he had an Evian and I did not.

He turned back to me, dark Clooney eyes dancing.

"Lucky," he said, raising his bottle in a toast. "You should see our receptionist down at Velman. Like a reject from the ugly factory. You two, you know?"

"She's in a serious relationship with a firefighter."

"Well, that makes sense. For she surely is *hot*."

He managed to chuckle heartily while taking a long pull from the bottle, reminding me of that old ventriloquist trick.

"This is terrific," I said to change the subject. "Always nice to meet a fellow traveler."

"Oh, there's plenty of slop in the trough to go around," he said. He adjusted his tie to make it lie equidistant between his lapels. I wasn't wearing a tie and hadn't worn one for over a year, since the day of my mom's funeral. So I tugged at the right sleeve of my sport coat to make it even with the left sleeve. His analogy bothered me. I had compared my calling to the knightly quests of yore. Now I was the runt pig slurping the big hogs' dregs.

"How *is* business, Teddy? Can I call you Teddy?"

"Anybody can," I said.

"Hey, my friends call me Dres."

"That's terrific, Mr. Falks," I said.

He unloaded the full weight of his smile upon me. I smiled back. We sat there for a pregnant moment, smiling at each other.

"You've been hired by Katrina Bates," he said through his perfect teeth.

"Says who?"

"Says my client."

"Who is Tom Bates."

Smile.

"Makes you wonder why Tom thinks that," I said.

"PI One oh one, Ted: If you're gonna contact the target, block your number first."

"What if I said I don't know what the heck you're talking about?"

"Then I'd ask how you knew Tom's name just now. And I'd probably show you these."

He pulled a stack of four-by-six glossies from his pocket and slid it across the blotter toward me. There I was with Katrina, buying Italian ices from the Mexican. Then the two of us strolling by the river, my right arm fully extended at the back end of Archie's leash. There we were on the bench, with the hospital a blurry monolith in the background. The next sequence included me sitting in my car in front of Kinsey Brock's apartment on Seventeenth Street, loitering outside the Rock Gym on Kingston Pike, where she worked out, leaning on the brick wall of the Copper Cellar on the Strip while she ate lunch with a couple of girlfriends.

"Looks like I've been outclassed," I said.

"Outgunned," he said.

"That, too," I said.

"We got a situation here, Ted."

"I can't tell you why she hired me, Dres."

"I'm not asking you to. I already know why. You told my client and then you followed the girl."

"Is it his girl?"

Smile.

"Not that it matters now," I said. "She fired me."

"The Hurricane?"

"Huh?"

"Sorry. That's what we call her down at the firm."

"Seems mean."

"Guess she hired you to be her FEMA."

"That would make sense if you called her New Orleans. But I've been fired, so really my snout's out of that trough."

He nodded. "I know."

"How do you know?" I pictured him crouched behind a bush with one of those high-tech listening devices trained at our bench.

"The Big Easy fessed up. 'Big Easy,' get it? Tom goes right to the source, asks her point-blank, 'Who is this Ruzak and why is he raggin' on me?' So Easy tells him who and why, most of which he already knew from us, except the firing part, which she also told him. But you win some and you lose some, right, Ted?"

"Right," I said. "Usually more of one than the other. Anyway, like I said, Dres, I don't have a dog in this fight anymore. You've got the pictures and Katrina's confession, so I'm kind of at a loss right now trying to understand why you're here with the slightly menacing attitude."

"'Menacing'? My attitude is *menacing*?"

"Leaning toward the confrontational."

"Just establishing the context, Ted. Putting all the cards on the table." He polished off his Evian and placed the sweating empty beside the cocktail napkin. Not on it, beside it. Then he drew a long white envelope from his breast pocket and dropped it on top of the pile of pictures.

"What's this?" I asked.

"Five thousand dollars. Cash."

"The Velman Group wants to hire a detective?"

"No, we want to buy the file."

"What file?"

"Or rent it. We'll give it back."

"The Bates file."

He nodded. "That file."

I thought about that.

"There is no Bates file," I said.

"No Bates file?"

I shook my head. "I destroy my old files."

"Teddy, you must've forgotten who you're talking to. No dick in his right mind destroys his files. Information is our lifeblood."

"Unless it's useless information."

"No such thing, in my experience."

"Well, that's probably more extensive than mine. But that's my policy."

"What's your policy?"

"File destruction. When the case ends, so does the file."

"Maybe for another five you could 'reconstruct' it?"

"What, like tape all the shredded strips back together?"

"Hey, the means is all up to you, Ted. We'd just like to buy that file."

"Which raises a question, Dres."

"Our client is a very private man. The thought of personal information floating around out there is intolerable to him. Because who knows what could happen, right? Plus, he's also a very successful man, and you don't get to be where Tom Bates is without making a few enemies along the way, right? It's an unacceptable risk to a man like our client, having some potentially very damaging and very embarrassing information in the hands of a total stranger who's already demonstrated his disregard of the old saw that discretion is the better part of valor. So I can go to ten, but that's the bottom line, Ted. That's the final offer; take it or leave it."

"Take it or leave it, or . . . what?"

"We're both professionals, Ted. We understand how it works, right?"

"To be totally honest with you, Dres, I'm not sure either proposition is entirely accurate."

I slid the bulging white envelope toward his side of the desk.

"Even if I still had the file—which I don't—it's not for sale. I may be licenseless, but I'm not licentious."

Smile. His, not mine.

SCENE SEVEN
The Office

Moments Later

*F*elicia dropped the Bates file on top of the surveillance photos and slid into the chair vacated by Dresden Falks. She flipped her hair over her collar and I caught a whiff of Chanel. Chanel, on a secretary's salary, but then, she did live with Bob, who might have given it to her for Christmas or maybe her birthday.

"When is your birthday?" I asked her.

"November nineteenth, why?"

"I never knew."

"You never asked."

"I would have gotten you something."

"Little late now."

"Somebody's nervous," I said, tapping the folder before me.

"Extremely."

"Ten grand," I said, thinking that would buy a heck of a lot of perfume, but saying, "for what?"

"Maybe he's a sadistic serial killer and he's afraid she's told you what's going on in the basement."

She caught me looking at the Evian bottle, picked it up, wiped the sweat ring from the mahogany with the unused napkin. The tension in my shoulders eased.

I said, "He's got boocoos of it; it means nothing to him; maybe to him ten grand is like offering me a buck fifty."

"I don't follow."

"Maybe the amount seems like a lot for a little to us, while to him it's a little for a lot."

"A lot of what?"

"Don't know," I said. "But that's not the salient point."

"Seems pretty salient to me."

"She didn't divulge any dark, dirty secrets, nothing that would get him into trouble, beyond the infidelity, which is trouble, but not serious trouble. Not ten thousand dollars' worth."

"A fact he's not aware of."

"Right. Hence the offer."

"I love it when you use words like *hence* and *salient*. It makes me feel like we're involved in something important."

"And even the compulsive cheating is an open secret in their milieu."

"See, there you go again: 'milieu.'"

"Katrina would know."

"Ruzak, I'm going to point out a couple of things. First, you're probably right and Tom thinks you probably do know, but she didn't at the most likely time when she would. Second, there is no case. She fired you."

"I think that's the point," I said.

"I *know* that's the point."

"About Katrina. She knows something or he thinks she knows something or might know something, and that something is something nobody else is supposed to know, which has made him very, very nervous."

"She's in danger?"

"Could be."

"We're back to the knight-in-shining-armor shtick, aren't we?"

"You shouldn't demean it, Felicia. The world could use a few of those."

"Ruzak, do you have a crush on Katrina Bates?"

"I'm a professional," I said, echoing Dresden Falks.

"It's okay, you know," she said. "Look at Lancelot and Guinevere."

"That would make Tom Bates King Arthur."

"Makes more sense than casting you as Lancelot."

"Why do you pick on me?" I asked. "What's the payoff?"

The phone rang. She didn't move to answer it, which was sort of her job—okay, it *was* her job. I grabbed the receiver.

"This is Ruzak," I said.

I hung up two minutes later. She still hadn't moved. When I was a security guard working the night shift at the bank and she was a waitress at the Old City Diner, I would try in my own awkward way to get her to ignore her other tables and talk to me. But I spent more time watching the back of her head and those well-developed calves than any other part of her. Then I hired her away from that job to be my secretary without even knowing if she could type. It didn't take a genius to figure out why. At the time, I didn't know she had a boyfriend named Bob. I had never met Bob, but I knew he was a firefighter, and it was chiefly for that reason I pictured him with features similar to my old G.I. Joe dolls packed in a box sitting in my hall closet. Mom kept everything.

"Dresden Falks," I said. "They're doubling the offer."

She gave a low whistle. "Twenty grand."

"That's about five thousand dollars per page."

"You should take it."

"Why? Lancelot wouldn't."

"There's nothing damning in it, right? So who gets hurt except the cheating asshole who's ponying up? Plus, you'll have the satisfaction of cutting Mr. Genius down to size."

"Make him feel like a sap."

I tensed, waiting for it: "And he's not used to feeling that way, unlike you," or something along those lines.

But she said, "And it's about the only thing you can do to protect her. He gets the file and sees there's nothing harmful in it."

"Unless he thinks I've redacted the harmful stuff."

"So put something harmful in there."

I thought about that. Then I said, "Huh?"

"Make something up. Something outrageous, ridiculous. Stick it in the file. He'll know it isn't true, but he'll assume you think it is. He'll think if you left *that* in, you didn't take anything else out."

"That's so . . ." I searched for the word.

"Diabolical?"

"Byzantine. What about the ethical obligation to my client?"

"You don't have a client, Ruzak."

"Still, I should tell her about the offer. What I may or may not pass off might be bogus, but the offer isn't. The desperation to know what's in the file isn't. Tom Bates has something to hide, and whatever that something is, it goes beyond a little extracurricular activity."

"Not your business, Ruzak."

"I guess not in the professional sense."

"Is there any other kind?"

"Yes," I said. "The human kind."

SCENE EIGHT
Old City Diner

Two Days Later

Twenty thousand dollars?" Katrina Bates asked. She removed her Chanel shades and rubbed her eyes. They were puffy, as if she had been crying or not sleeping well. "For what?"

We were sitting in the booth farthest from the door, the same booth I had sat in while trying to make time with the woman who one day I would pay to answer phones, type letters, mail invoices, and mock me. It was the perfect location to keep an eye on the door, and I wanted to keep an eye on the door because I was certain Katrina Bates was being followed. You don't get to be the largest private investigation company in three states by slacking off on the details. I arrived a few minutes before she did, and had drawn the blinds so no Velmanistas could snap off a few through the window while we talked.

"That's something I'd like to know," I said.

Our waitress, a corpulent specimen named Lila, swung by to warm up our coffee. She asked how Felicia was doing. They missed her. I said she was doing great, and she said she had heard the state was shutting me down again because I had flunked the PI test, again. I said that didn't matter, the flunking part, because technically speaking, I wasn't a detective; I was an analyst. Then she got snide and said that instead of calling myself one, maybe I should go see one. My first instinct was to blurt "Oh, yeah, fat ass?" But I didn't. What would be the point?

Katrina watched me empty two packets of artificial sweetener and two of those little plastic containers of cream into my coffee.

"Do you know when I first realized I loved Tom? On our second date, we met for coffee and he took it black."

"Not many men do."

"I thought it was so . . . masculine."

Ergo, not many men are masculine. I stirred my coffee. Sipped. Fought the irrational urge to extend my pinkie.

"That's the thing about Tom," she said. "He's overloaded with testosterone. The quintessence of manliness."

"Like feeling up the waitress on his honeymoon."

"He always reminded me of a Kennedy. You know, all that earthiness and energy. All that physical and cerebral *franticness*. The sense that every *second* is precious, not to be wasted, *sinful* to waste."

She sipped her undiluted coffee.

"I don't know if that's the secret to all success, but it certainly is the secret of his. His father was only forty-six when he died, Tom's grandfather fifty-two, and Tom's always been convinced he is going to die young, like them."

"Life is a cup to be drunk to its very dregs," I said.

"Is that a quote?"

"I'm not sure," I replied. "Sometimes I say things that sound like they might be, and they very well might be, only I've forgotten where I heard it or read it and I think maybe it's original."

She laughed. "Well, Teddy, *you* certainly are."

"So this offer is just another manifestation of Tom's cerebral franticness? He's covering all the bases?"

"He's an honest man, Teddy. I'm not saying he's never fudged on his taxes or told his share of white lies, and you already know about the affairs, but he's no criminal."

"That you know of."

"We've been married for twenty years. I *would* know."

"Okay. Why would someone with nothing to hide be willing to pay twenty thousand dollars for something that would only confirm he has nothing to hide? And if he has nothing to hide, what makes you think you could destroy him with it?"

"Who said I wanted to destroy him?"

"You did. On the phone the day I called him." I opened the file and showed her my note, which read "Wants to destroy him."

She studied it for a few seconds, and then she said, "I hope you take that part out before you give it to him."

"So it's okay? You don't care?"

She shrugged. Tears formed in the corners of her eyes.

"He's moved out," she said. "I think he's shacking up with that little whore."

"Kinsey Brock?"

"Or some other little whore. What does it matter which little whore?"

"So you don't think he'll confront you about it?"

"About what? He's the one shacking up."

"About what's in the file."

"You're worried about me. That's sweet."

"I haven't been married to him for twenty years. I don't know him like you do. And maybe you don't know him, not like you think you do. I don't know what's in his past or what kind of paranoia could make somebody offer twenty grand for something his wife already knows. What I do know is that if I accept his offer, I'm going to cover my own bases. I'm going to prepare for every contingency, or at least every contingency that comes to mind."

I told her about the plan to insert the bogus allegation.

"That way, he'll be convinced I've given all I got. And I'll do it in such a way that he won't think it came from you. He'll think I got it independently."

"Why does that matter?"

"It matters for the same reason I've been maneuvered into selling him the file. Because you could be wrong. You might not know him like you think you know him."

"And if you don't sell him the file, he might think I actually do know or you actually do, and somebody might get hurt to protect his secret—is that what you're saying?"

I nodded. "There's no way around it now. They don't buy my story it's been destroyed. Selling it—and the big lie in it—might be the only thing that buys your safety."

"And that matters to you?"

"Of course it matters to me, Katrina."

"Oh my. Say my name again."

"Katrina," I said.

"I like the way you say it," she said.

SCENE NINE
The Sterchi Building

That Evening

Whittaker intercepted me in the lobby. I wasn't sure, but I thought he was wearing the same suit as the day he confronted me about Archie. He was like a cartoon character—always in the same clothes.

"Mr. Ruzak," he said.

"Whittaker," I said. I wasn't sure if Whittaker was his first or his last name. "My thirty days aren't up yet."

"We've received reports of a strong odor."

"What kind of odor?"

"The odor of feces."

"From my apartment? Have you checked the plumbing? My dog does all his business outdoors."

"I would think that's something you'd be highly motivated to lie about."

"You're calling me a liar?"

"I'm saying the smell of poop on the third floor is unmistakable."

"You've smelled it?"

"I've had reports, as I believe I've told you."

He shadowed me to the elevators. I had my briefcase. I figured I could coldcock him with it. Just lay it upside his head. No witnesses, his word against mine.

"It could be flatulence," I offered. "His farts are extremely loud and incredibly close."

"Why are you smiling?" he asked.

"Sorry. I've never outgrown it. Words like *fart* and *poop*. *Titties* to a lesser degree. Tickles me even if I'm the one who says it. Fart."

He stared at me, stone-faced.

"I was wondering if management ever made exceptions to the no-pet clause," I said.

"Do you have a disability? Are you blind, Mr. Ruzak?"

"In what sense?"

His smile was as tight as his Windsor knot.

"No, the management does not," he said.

"What about some sort of damage-deposit arrangement? Say a month's rent."

"If I make an exception for one tenant—"

"Two months. In cash."

"Mr. Ruzak, are you offering me a bribe?"

"I just want what's fair. For you, for me, for the dog."

"Maybe you should have thought of that before you got the dog."

The doors slid open. I didn't step inside. He'd just follow me.

"Well, I've put an ad in the paper. Hopefully I'll find him a good home before the thirty days is up."

"The dog must be vacated from the premises, whether you find a good home for it or not."

"Do you have a dog?" I asked. The doors slid closed. That bothered him; I could tell. *Why didn't Ruzak get on that car?* He went shifty-eyed on me.

"I own," he said stiffly. "I don't rent."

"So you do have a dog?"

"I didn't say that."

"Why are you avoiding the question?"

"Why are you avoiding the issue?"

"My mom died," I said.

"Excuse me?"

"And my dad. I have no brothers or sisters or any family close by. I'm what you'd call between relationships right now. Are you alone, Whittaker?"

"That's none of your business, Ruzak."

So maybe Whittaker was his last name and he was going tit for tat with the "Ruzak."

"You're asking me to get rid of more than a dog; that's all I'm saying."

"I'm not concerned about your personal problems."

"Well, it sure would be a better world if more of us were, don't you think?"

I hit the button. The elevator hadn't moved. The doors opened.

"Are you going up?" I asked. "Or down?"

"I could take that as a threat."

"Take it however you want," I said as the doors closed. I called out as I rose, "And he doesn't poop in the apartment!"

I couldn't detect any noxious fumes on my floor. I dropped to my hands and knees outside my door and sniffed near the crack. Nothing. I stood up and announced out loud in the empty hallway, "There is no poop." I was more righteously indignant than I had a right to be. The issue wasn't unauthorized defecation; the

issue was the unauthorized defecator. Still, it bordered on harassment, giving me thirty days, then hounding me over trumped-up
charges of illegal dumping. It got my back up. It made me want to
fight. *Damn you and your Paragraph F, Section Five, Whittaker!*

After his walk, Archie removed himself to the far corner of the
family room and stretched out on his belly, working on a rawhide
chewy while I put the water on to boil for pasta and fried up a
pound of ground chuck for the sauce. Even the smell of food
couldn't entice him to be near me. There he sprawled on the far
side of the apartment, completely indifferent, not only to the smell
of meat, which was hard to understand, but to the struggles of his
owner on his behalf. People get pets for their companionship, and
I suspected most people get dogs partly because their species'
slavish devotion to us is deeply gratifying. To feel needed might
not be as primal a drive as sex or hunger, but there was no doubt in
my mind it excites more than a few neurons in our insula. I caught
this show about people who "adopt" monkeys to be their surrogate
children. They construct special rooms for them, a kind of monkey nursery; they diaper them, push them around in strollers, take
them to the playground, prop them up at the dinner table in high
chairs, dress them in baby clothes, and pepper them with baby
talk. The reporter actually said this about one woman who spent
thousands of dollars on one of these creatures: "Since she was a
little girl, she had dreamed of owning a monkey." After all that
money and seven years of his mommy taking care of his every
need, this creature (a capuchin monkey from South America),
turned on her with his two-inch canines and nearly ripped her
scalp off. Talk about ingratitude! Off she sent him to the monkey
farm. Yet there she was on a visit a couple years later, crying outside his enclosure, trying to get his attention: "Mommy's here,
Jack. Hello, Jack. Come say hello to Mommy, Jack." While the

monkey pointedly, in my opinion, ignored her. I didn't know whether to feel sorry for the monkey (who had, after all, been ripped away from his real mommy, stuffed in a wooden crate, shipped several thousand miles, and forced to live for seven years in a diaper, with no monkey friends to play with) or feel sorry for the woman, who was capable of bearing children, according to the reporter, but instead chose to lavish her maternal gifts on a wild animal that no amount of cuddling could domesticate. I suspected there was something a bit more profound at work in her than a simple childhood dream; all those years and all those thousands of dollars would have been better spent on a good therapist.

Felicia called midway through *Wheel of Fortune*.

"Well, did you get the green light?"

"I did. How old do you think Pat Sajak is?"

"Who?"

"He's been on this show forever. I thought he was old back when I was a kid, and I'm a long way from being a kid now." And Vanna White, a woman her age still wearing evening gowns. Each year it was a little creepier, like one of those aging Disney villainesses, the plunging necklines and the frozen, slightly ghoulish, too-big-for-the-face smile.

"Ruzak, turn off the damned TV and talk to me."

I turned off the damned TV. The ensuing silence was thundering.

"What did she say?" Felicia asked.

"She said he was as pure as the driven snow, so I should feel free to muddy him up a bit."

"She's not afraid of catching hell?"

"He moved out."

"Why?"

"I guess to shack up with the little whore."

"'Little whore?'"

"Katrina's term."

"So what did you come up with?"

"I didn't, but if I had, it would have been something less pejorative, like the 'other woman.'"

"No, Ruzak. The big lie."

"Oh. I haven't yet."

"But you're working on it between buying vowels?"

"Well, I keep going back and forth. I mean, we don't want to cross too far into slanderous territory. A felony would be better than a misdemeanor—we're going for big, after all—but you don't want something too serious, like child molestation or serial killing. And I don't want anything connected to Katrina, like poisoning her soup or deliberately giving her an STD."

"How about drugs? He has a cocaine habit."

"Drugs would be good, but maybe something nastier than cocaine. Meth or OxyContin."

"Heroin."

"Hard to stay a functioning overachiever on heroin."

"It's a lie, Ruzak," she reminded me.

"But the best ones have their own internal logic. Maybe we should go with something more exotic, I don't know, a little less banal than drug addiction."

"Tell an addict it's banal."

"You know what I meant."

Archie rose from the spot he hadn't moved from since I let him out of his crate, took two steps toward the sofa, upon which I lay beached, then froze, as if startled that I was still in the room (*Why hasn't this palooka left yet?*). He stared at me, the soggy remnants of the chewy jutting from his mouth.

"Here's what we do," I said. "I give Archie to Tommy."

"Give what to who?"

"Not for real. Bob's allergic, I know. But I tell Whittaker I've gotten rid of him, and anytime he pops in unannounced and finds him, I say, 'Oh, I'm just pet-sitting.'"

"Ruzak, one of us has lost hold of this conversation, and I don't think it's me."

"There's no prohibition against it. The lease is completely silent on the issue."

"Oh. You've been busted."

"Whittaker won't buy it, though. It could come down to some kind of eviction proceeding and they might put Tommy on the stand. I wouldn't want to do that to a little kid, make him lie like that. Maybe if we convinced him I really *did* give him the dog, only I have to keep him because Bob's allergic. Bob could testify to that. Do you think Bob would have a problem doing that? Not telling the truth, but going to bat for me, since we've never officially met?"

"Why don't we apply the lesson we learned from high school biology, Ruzak."

"What lesson? The only thing I remember is the innards of a baby pig make me nauseated."

"Nature prefers the simple to the complex."

"I don't remember learning that."

"That's obvious to anyone who's listened to you for five minutes. You have this tendency to muck up the works with too much information. It's like your brain is on constant overload. Get rid of the dog, Ruzak."

"You think I should?"

"He doesn't like you."

Spoken so bluntly, the truth hit like a slam in the solar plexus.

I didn't argue with her, though. She knew the situation too well and, more important, she knew me too well.

"Maybe he just needs a little more time," I said, and I wondered if that woman from the monkey report had thought the same thing. *Jack just needs a little more time to get adjusted.* And then the damn thing nearly ripped the top of her head off.

"You should apply the same principle to the Bates case," she said. "Keep it simple. Simple and plausible."

"I thought we were going for outrageous."

"Go too far and he'll know what you're up to. He doesn't know you like I know you, and he'll assume no detective would bother putting something so outlandish in a case file."

"Maybe not something criminal," I mused aloud. "Something embarrassing."

"Impotency."

"Homosexuality."

"Who's embarrassed by that anymore?"

"When I was a kid, we called them 'homos.'"

She laughed, for some reason.

"A different kink. . . . He's into animals," she said.

"Monkeys."

"Monkeys?"

"All his life, he's dreamed of having a monkey."

"That's really sick. I had no idea your mind worked that way."

"I was thinking about them earlier."

"Oh my God!"

"Not in that way."

"I'm not going to ask why."

"It breaks the plausibility rule," I said. "Who's going to believe a Nobel finalist sodomizes lower primates?"

"We're the randiest species on earth, Ruzak. A guy will stick his doohickey into practically anything with an orifice."

"And some things without one." *Doohickey?* "I've heard of farm-workers in the watermelon patch."

"Let's move on to something else."

"Illegitimate children."

"Plagiarism."

"Internet porn."

"Gambling."

"Necrophilia."

"With dead monkeys."

By this point, we were both laughing so hard, talking was impossible. Who knew character assassination could be such fun?

SCENE TEN
Outside the Ely Building

Two Days Later

*T*he little guy with the square head and round spectacles fell into step beside me on the sidewalk, and I thought of Whittaker lunging from the shadows in the lobby of the Sterchi. Why was I being bushwhacked so much lately?

"Mr. Ruzak," he said.

"Mr. Hinton," I said.

"All done with the research for the day?"

"Here's something that might help your kid: Napoléon loved ice-skating."

"He's already turned in his report, but I appreciate it."

"Anything I can do."

"Mr. Ruzak, I'm not trying to hurt or deny anyone their God-given right to make a living in this country."

"Glad to hear it."

"And I have an obligation to the taxpayers of this state to pursue matters in the most judicious and financially prudent way possible."

"Oh." I got it. "You'd rather I voluntarily shut my doors."

"Best for everyone all around." He seemed pleasantly surprised I got it.

"I'm curious. How did you know I had a client named Katrina Bates?"

"She's not your client," he reminded me.

"Okay. How did you know I had a nonclient named Katrina Bates?"

"Let's say I have my sources."

Those were finite. We weren't even to the end of the block before I placed my bet.

"Dresden Falks of the Velman Group."

He answered with a small conspiratorial smile.

"I'm hurt," I said. "I thought he was my new BFF."

"'BFF'?"

"Ask your tenth grader. Who else have you contacted?"

"I've told you too much already, Mr. Ruzak. It's an ongoing investigation."

"Unlike my business."

"Since you're so dead set on it, perhaps you might think of obtaining your license in another state."

"Relocate."

"There must be at least one or two with standards a little less rigorous than the state of Tennessee's."

We stopped at the corner. Across the street, a middle-aged couple sat at a small metal patio table in the fenced-in courtyard of the Hilton, sipping grandes from the Starbucks kiosk in the lobby. They were decked out in biker gear: black leather jackets, chrome chains, jackboots. The guy's hair was streaked with gray and fell down the middle of his back in a ponytail. Hers was platinum blond, laced with purple, cut short, and spiked with gel. You don't normally think of hard-core bikers whiling away a spring afternoon sipping lattes from Starbucks.

"But I love Knoxville," I said. "Knoxville is my home."

"So much of life comes down to that, though, doesn't it? Choosing between two conflicting loves."

"Wow. That's pretty deep. Who said that?"

"I don't know that anyone did."

I nodded. "I'm the same way."

He followed me through the intersection and fell about a half step behind as my stride lengthened—I had about fourteen inches on him—puffing in the slightly humid air as he broke into a semitrot to keep up. We walked past the main branch of the library, and I thought of intersections, the strange serendipity that sometimes arises between thought and symbol. It wasn't a very productive line of thought—few of mine were—and a disinterested observer might come to the conclusion that I either read too much or not quite enough.

"Happens all the time," I said. "I think or say something that sounds like something someone really ought to write down, and I get all excited, because it's tough after ten thousand years of human history to even have an original thought, only to find out later somebody else said pretty much the same thing two hundred years ago, and I don't know if I'm parroting them or just had the same thought independently. Like the whole concept of truth, Mr. Hinton. You know what the most haunting question in the Bible is? When Pilate says to Jesus, 'What is the truth?' You know, is it empirical and objective, or is it all relative and subjective? Is my truth your truth? Or is truth something outside both of us, immutable as the atomic weight of lithium? When you think about it, all science, religion, philosophy, morals, everything, turns on Pilate's question. What is the truth?"

Now, standing on the corner of Church and Henley, waiting for the light to change, Hinton said, slightly out of breath, "All right, then. I'll bite. What is the truth, Mr. Ruzak?"

"Boy," I said. "You got me."

The light changed. I strode, he trotted, and I wondered if he intended to keep this up until he collapsed in a winded heap at my feet.

"It's all I can do to keep my head above the existential water," I confessed. "But I try to do the right thing. You won't believe this, but that's always been very important to me, from a very early age, doing the right thing. Get it from my mom. I'll give you an example. One summer we drove up to Gatlinburg to spend a few days at the park, and Mom bought this kitschy souvenir from one of those touristy shops along the main drag. I don't remember what it was, something like a paperweight with the mountains inside, or it might have been the trip when she finally broke down and bought me the dream catcher. I was going through my nightmare phase, at least two or three a week. Not that Mom believed it would actually work; that wasn't the point; *I* thought it did. You know, magical thinking. Anyway, we're back home and she looks at the receipt and discovers they undercharged her twelve cents. So you know what she did? She wrote a check for twelve cents and mailed it to the store. My dad, who wasn't a stickler like her when it came to morality—he was a salesman, after all— pointed out the stamp cost more than the check, but that wasn't Mom's point. She even stuck a note in there kind of lecturing the owner that twelve cents might not seem like much, but if he undercharged every customer twelve cents on everything he sold, eventually he'd lose his business."

"What do you think your mother would say, Mr. Ruzak, about your current situation?"

"I don't think she'd be entirely pleased, but that's a particular misery, constantly trying to live up to your parents' ideals. You're doomed to failure."

At the corner of Henley and Summit Hill, he said querulously, "How far away from your office do you normally park?"

"Oh, I'm not going to my car."

"No? Then where are you going? Not the Sterchi Building."

"How do you know I live at the Sterchi Building?"

He didn't answer. I was thinking, *Now this is a pretty thorough guy, for a bureaucrat.* Javert to my Jean Valjean. Maybe if I reversed course and followed Henley to the bridge, he'd jump into the river.

"I have an errand to run down on Broadway," I said.

"Broadway!" he practically whined. "You're walking all the way to Broadway?" He was aghast. You would have thought I told him I was shuffling on my knees to St. Peter's Square.

"I need to work off some of the winter pounds."

He pulled the white handkerchief from his lapel pocket and mopped his brow. "I left my hat in the car."

"You don't have to come," I said. "A harder man might consider this a sort of benign harassment."

"I was hoping we could reach an understanding, Mr. Ruzak."

"I've always been one hundred percent for that, Mr. Hinton."

"Why put off the inevitable?"

"Basic human nature?"

"You're not stupid; you must know it's only a matter of time."

"But, see, I'm an optimist. I hope for the best in everything."

"That's not optimism," he protested, and, unable to help himself, gave my sleeve a little tug. "That's wearing blinders."

I glanced down at his face and noticed the smudges on his spectacles, the strayed eyelash clinging to one lens, and for the first time I saw Walter Hinton as the scrawny four-eyed kid getting picked on by some sandbox tyrant twice his size, heard the taunts of little girls whose cruelty at that age had no boundaries, felt it slam down hard into the marrow of my empathetic bones: *I'll fix you one day; I'll fix all of you. . . . One day, I'll be in* law enforcement! Pity usually worked on me as a call to action, but what could I do? The only thing he wanted from me was the termination of my career. Not even the poor guy by the side of the road asked that of the Good Samaritan. *Hey, thanks for saving my life, now, by the way, renounce your Samaritan citizenship.* It also struck me, and not without a tinge of resentment, that the psychiatrists and evolutionary biologists had it tamped down tighter than your aunt Tilly's brassiere: Our life's course is determined at a very early age; between our genetics and our formation from one to about four, we don't have a snowball's chance in hell of self-determination, sort of the scientific equivalent of Calvinism.

"Well," I said. "That's what it comes down to, Walter. I do what I do, you do what you do, and we let the chips fall where they may."

His gray eyes malevolently danced behind his dirty lenses. Through thin lips he sneered, "I don't like you, Theodore Ruzak."

SCENE ELEVEN
The Lighthouse Mission

A Half Hour Later

*I*t was five o'clock and dinner service had just begun. Families gravitated to the tables near the plate-glass windows fronting Broadway; the singles more toward the middle and rear, where the buffet line and the battered stainless-steel urns filled with instant coffee were located. I waited my turn in line with everyone else. The director of the mission, a burly ex-marine named Walter Newberry (another Walter, another case of serendipity), stood over the steam table, ladling out the ground steak and mash potatoes and green beans, the sleeves of his white T-shirt rolled up to reveal his massive biceps and the *Semper Fi* tattoo on his left shoulder, while sweat rolled from his forehead and beads of it quivered on his upper lip. He greeted everyone by name, asked how they were doing, how their families—if they had family—were doing. "Hey, George, you're looking great! How's the AA going? How's your kid? He finish school finally?" He did a double take when my turn came.

"Ruzak? How ya doin', my brother?"

He stretched his arm over the sneeze guard and gave me the fist bump.

"Can't complain," I said. Of course, I could—there was plenty there—but being surrounded by homeless people gives you some perspective, a sense of proportion.

"Haven't seen you in awhile. What's it been, coupla months?"

"More like five."

"Business must be good."

"What there is."

"You look good. Like you lost a few pounds."

"It's the warm weather," I said. "So mostly what I lost were layers."

"Come down for a little work? Could use the extra hands."

"Can we talk first?"

"Kind of busy right now. Have a seat; be over when I can."

I took a seat at the end of a table, beside an old gentleman whose broken fingernails were encrusted with dirt and who gave me a brief congenial nod before diving back into his collards. I never cared for that southern delicacy; it always felt like I was consuming weeds.

I waited over an hour, sipping lukewarm Folgers from a Styrofoam cup, watching the shadow of the building stretch across Broadway as the sun set behind it. People came and went like the candy wrappers and remnants of plastic bags skittering along the empty street in the dying light. Most ate quickly and in silence, and then another pair of ragged shoes shuffled through the door and somebody else waited patiently at the end of the line for a hot meal and a moment or two of cool air. My table had turned over for the third time when Walter finally slid into the chair across from me, his face beet red and knuckles redder, looking like raw hamburger.

"You weren't hungry?" he asked. I shook my head. "Not pleasure, then. Business."

"Sort of," I said. I pulled the bulging white envelope from my breast pocket and slid it across the table. He lifted one edge of the flap with a fingernail and squinted inside.

"Sweet Jesus, Ruzak," he whispered.

"Twenty grand," I whispered back.

"What for?"

"For you. The mission."

"Shit. Why?"

"Let's just say I need the tax deduction."

"Well, all I can say is, business must be *really* good."

The envelope disappeared. He laid his enormous forearms on the table and studied my face.

"There's a catch," he said.

"No. It's yours. All yours. No strings, except maybe a higher grade of coffee."

"You don't like the coffee?"

"It sucks."

"I'll get the Starbucks."

"I'm not too keen on Starbucks." Not because of the taste so much as the creepy water goddess–like creature on all the cups. "You can get Dunkin' Donuts at the grocery now, but my favorite is Krispy Kreme."

He laughed, for some reason. "What else?"

"Nothing else. You do great work here. Important work. Work that matters."

"Meaning you ain't sure yours does."

"Meaning there is a string, but I'm the one tied to the other end of it."

"Free meals for life?"

"I'm serious; I don't want anything."

"You say you don't want anything, but you hand me twenty

grand in cash and sit there and don't move and talk about being tied to strings."

"I hate to donate and run."

"This some kind of blood money, Ruzak? And you want to sleep at night?"

"No, really, nothing like that. I'm pretty sure I'm doing the right thing. The dog I had in this fight fired me, and I don't even know the one I'm pulling a number on. It's all with the best intentions."

"And you're afraid you're paving your own road."

"Or someone else's. But if I didn't pave it, something bad might happen to them."

"Okay. Got it. Or I'll pretend I get it, because I consider you a friend, Ruzak. You got heart."

"It's just I don't . . . I don't . . . I don't . . . I don't want to live my life cowering in the shadow of my own fear; that's the thing. I want to walk in the light."

"I hear you, brother. Save the worries of tomorrow for tomorrow."

"But this is the second or third time I've paved this road," I admitted. "You know, thinking you're doing the right thing and then it blows up in your face."

"You gotta do that, Teddy. It comes with the territory. Just 'cause somebody can take a hatchet to it doesn't mean you can't stick your neck out."

"That's the idea," I said. "I can't save everybody, but maybe I can save the ones who fall into my little orbit."

He turned his gaze from me and allowed it to wander around the crowded room.

"Heard that, brother," he said. "Heard that."

"Amen," I said.

SCENE TWELVE
The Tomato Head Restaurant, Market Square

The Next Day

*A*bout six blocks from my apartment, a manageable walking distance in clement weather, was the Tomato Head restaurant in Market Square, serving a tasty variety of specialty pizzas and sandwiches (the roast beef with the blue cheese dressing was my favorite) and their trademark blue tortilla chips. There was patio seating on the square, but in the warmer months I preferred eating inside, where local artists displayed their paintings and collages (the cheapest one going for $150, but that included the matting and frame) and the steady thrum of conversation provided some distraction from the steady thrum of the monologue between my ears.

Something happened while I sat there, a rarity that never failed to startle me, like someone sneaking up and tapping me hard on the shoulder: My cell phone rang.

"I missed your call last night," Katrina Bates said.

"That's okay," I said.

She laughed, for some reason.

"Oh, *good*," she said.

"I just wanted to let you know the package has been delivered."

"Very good, Mr. Bond."

"And something else. Kinsey Brock is having an affair with Tom's best friend."

"Excuse me?"

"Tom's girlfriend is cheating on him."

"And you know this for sure?"

"I don't know it at all. That's the red herring I planted in the file. Of course, she really might be cheating with his best friend, though the odds of me hitting that nail on the head out of the blue are pretty long."

"Who is Tom's best friend?"

"Don't you know?"

"I'm asking how *you* know."

"I don't know."

"You don't know?"

"It doesn't matter if I know. I don't have to know."

What I actually wrote in the file, under the 'Miscellany' tab, was this: "K.B. having illicit liaison with BF. *Verified*. Undet./ unclear if target aware of same."

"Who is his best friend?" I asked.

"Probably Trace Michelson."

I jotted the name on my napkin.

"What made you decide to go with this?" she asked.

"Well, number one, it's not something that must have come from you. Number two, I didn't think you'd mind creating a little friction between Tom and Kinsey. Number three, it's not something that he can come back and sue either of us for slander about, and it's not so far in left field that it comes across as a deliberate falsehood thrown in the file to justify the payment. That would be number four."

She sighed. It must have been a pretty loud sigh, too, for me to hear it through the phone and over the din of the lunchtime crowd.

"I wish you had cleared this with me first, Teddy."

"I thought I had."

"I mean the red herring. Teddy, Trace Michelson is gay."

"Oh," I said, feeling my face grow hot. "Openly?"

"He's lived with the same partner for fifteen years."

"Well," I said. "This is not necessarily a bad thing."

"He'll know immediately it's a lie. Wouldn't that defeat the purpose and by definition make it a bad thing?"

"But he won't know it's *my* lie. He might think it's Kinsey's lie."

"You talked to Kinsey?"

"No. But he won't know that, and he might not believe her denial."

"Why would Kinsey lie in the first place? Why would she tell a total stranger anything about her sex life? And why would she name a partner who is undeniably homosexual?"

"You're right. His head must be really spinning right now."

"Well, *somebody's* head certainly is."

"My point is, he won't know if this is something she told me or something I observed or even something somebody else told me. It's equally plausible he won't interpret it as a lie, but as a mistake. That I just got it wrong. Misidentified Trace as the lover." Except I threw in that one pivotal word: *verified*. I gulped my iced tea, hoping to cool off the burning sensation in my cheeks.

"Six years into our marriage, Tom became convinced I was having an affair," she said. "I wasn't, but that little fact was completely irrelevant. Like a lot of cheating husbands, he could rationalize his behavior, while holding his wife to the strictest standards of fidelity. He followed me. He monitored my phone calls. He hired an obnoxious detective to shadow my every move. He threatened to divorce me, throw me out into the street without a penny, even hinted he might hurt me."

"Hurt you?" I asked. "Hurt you how?"

"Well, let's see. He said if I ever left him, he would throw hydrochloric acid in my face."

"Ouch. If that's a hint, I'd hate to know what you'd call a threat. So you're thinking . . . what? What are you thinking? That this might put Kinsey in a really bad spot?"

""I could care less what spot it puts that little slut in."

"Oh, good," I said, which struck me as an oddly inappropriate response. "Well, I thought I should let you know in case he says something about it. I don't want you to be blindsided."

"Why not?"

"That's a good question," I said.

"Followed by a lousy answer."

"You did fire me," I acknowledged. "But the Falks offer threw a monkey wrench into the works." Again with the monkeys. Why did they keep popping up? "Plus, I'm probably a little too softhearted for my own good. Sometimes for *anybody's* good."

"I don't need your pity, Mr. Ruzak."

"It's not pity per se," I protested. "More like this general sense of obligation to anyone going through a rough time."

"I'm going to be fine," she said, and her voice broke when she said it. "It's just I could deal with it a lot better if it was a meaningless fling like all the others. That's what hurts."

"How do you know it isn't, though? Meaningless."

"I found love poems in his sock drawer."

"To Kinsey?"

"No, to Trace Michelson, the gay guy. Jesus! Very bad poetry, which surprised me; Tom's a better writer than that. Extolling her virtues and singing praises to certain portions of her anatomy, and I'm not talking about her eyes and hair."

"That's what I don't get," I said. "If he was so much in love, why did he wait until my call to leave you for her?"

"How the hell should I know? He's a fucking man. Maybe it's called having your cake and eating it, too."

"We're not monogamous by nature," I said, careful not to sound too defensive. "It's sort of an artificial construct."

"Weird. You don't know how much you sounded like Tom just now."

I felt strangely flattered. "Well," I said. "I do happen to be an effing man."

She laughed too long and too loud.

"Where are you right now?" she asked. "I hear people talking."

"The Tomato Head in Market Square."

"By yourself?"

"Uh-huh."

"I'll be there in fifteen minutes," she said. "Tom's on his way over to pick up some of his things and I don't want to be here when he does." She hung up before I could say anything, not that I had anything in particular to say.

My food came. I was used to eating alone, but I didn't think Katrina Bates was, so I decided to wait until she came so she wouldn't have to. The waiter came by and refilled my iced tea. A couple of tables turned over. Twenty minutes went by and still no Katrina. My roast beef sandwich rested before me, at once beckoning and forlorn. *Eat me, Ruzak, eat me.* I nibbled on some tortilla chips. I started to dial her cell number, then stopped. Maybe she'd changed her mind. Maybe Tom had showed up and she'd gotten waylaid. I figured maybe I should eat my sandwich before my blue cheese dressing went bad and gave me botulism. It was one thing to risk serious gastrointestinal complications for a dear friend or for a loyal secretary and coconspirator in my illegal detection operation, like Felicia; it was quite another to risk it for someone I hardly knew and who had fired me besides, cutting off an important cash conduit to fund my illegal detection operation.

So, not knowing what to do after another ten minutes had passed, I called Felicia and explained my dilemma.

"I would eat my sandwich and go," she said. "What do you owe Katrina Bates?"

"I just don't want to heap yet another one on her."

"Heap another what?"

"Rejection."

"Oh, brother. Are you aspiring to sainthood, Ruzak?"

"I'm not Catholic," I said. "Dad was, but Mom would rather have slit her Baptist wrists than see me receive the Sacrament. But I think I read somewhere you don't have to be Catholic to get the nod. And that makes sense in the theological scheme of things. God doesn't play favorites, you know, causing the rain to fall upon the just but not the just. But you could also argue that by God, God does. Look at Moses and David and all those other reluctant prophets and kings."

"Why do you do that? Why do you take every question so seriously, like you're being interviewed by *Time* magazine?"

"Maybe it's practice. Because I'm hoping, deep down, at some point, I might be newsworthy enough to be interviewed by *Time* magazine."

"That reminds me. *Time* magazine called. They want to interview you."

"Okay. Some things we should keep to ourselves." I looked at my watch. Thirty minutes now. The lunch crowd was thinning out. The waiter came by with my fourth refill. By this point, between the sugar and the caffeine, my head and stomach were feeling bloated and soggy.

"Call her," Felicia said. "Explain it's nothing personal, but you've got to get back to the office. You have important work to do for people who still happen to be your clients. Nothing personal. No offense."

"Have you noticed that?" I asked. "When somebody is about to say something guaranteed to offend you, the person always prefaces it with 'No offense, but . . .'?"

"No, I never noticed, but now I know and it'll come in handy, knowing that. . . . Oh, Ruzak?"

"Yeah?"

"No offense, but maybe you're not staying there out of the goodness of your heart, but out of the yearning of your loins."

"I don't find her attractive," I protested. "She's too . . ." I conjured up a mental picture of Katrina Bates. What was excessive? "Too coarse."

"'Coarse'?"

"She uses the *F* word. And she makes references to wick dipping."

Felicia laughed, for some reason. "Has it ever occurred to you, Ruzak, that you might be just a tad too tender for detective work? Don't answer that," she added quickly. "Forget I asked."

"And something else," I said. "The lie."

"Whose lie?"

"The file's lie. 'K.B. having illicit liaison with BF.' It didn't hit me until after I gave the file to Dresden Falks that 'K.B.' could be interpreted or *mis*interpreted as Katrina Bates. It didn't occur to me; now it's too late. He could think I meant his wife, not his girlfriend."

"So?"

"So Katrina said he threatened her before when he thought she was having an affair."

"Threatened her how?"

"With acid, and there's this, not her so much as a principle I was talking about just yesterday. You can't save everybody, but you can refrain from hurting people. You can add your light to the sum of light."

"Jesus?"

"No. I think it was the guy who wrote *War and Peace*."

"You've read *War and Peace*?"

"That would surprise you?"

"So you haven't read *War and Peace*."

"How do you know?"

"Because if you had, you would have said 'Yes, Felicia, as a matter of fact, I have read *War and Peace*.'"

"Maybe I reacted to the implication there that somehow not reading *War and Peace* diminishes me as a human being."

"That was an inference," she said. "You just didn't strike me as a *War and Peace* kind of guy."

"Well, I am."

"So you did read it."

"I didn't say that."

"You have it in you. You have the potentiality for it. If there's anybody who hasn't read it but who's an excellent candidate to one day read it, it would be you."

"Right," I said. "Something along those lines."

"I'm hanging up, Ruzak. Finish your sandwich and get back to the office. Screw Katrina Bates."

Maybe it was hunger, maybe the combination of caffeine and sugar, or maybe the fact that I was talking to Felicia, but I echoed, "'Screw Katrina Bates'?"

"I was going to say 'Fuck her,' but then you might think I'm coarse."

ACT TWO

The Victim

SCENE ONE
Sequoia Hills

That Evening

The house was brick, three stories of ivy-draped crimson in the Federal style, constructed on a gentle rise of land at the end of a cul-de-sac, behind a half wall of mortared Tennessee river rock, probably trucked in at great expense from the Little Pigeon in the Smokies. The windows were high and narrow, the shutters painted either black or forest green; it was hard to tell by the single streetlight. The grounds were immaculate: mature dogwood, maple, and Bradford pear, azaleas and daylilies and rhododendrons (which always reminded me of my mom, since they bloomed around Mother's Day), and, in the walk leading from the little metal gate in the stone wall to the front door, a fountain whose gurgle and splash I could hear inside my car, which was parked two hundred feet away.

"Nice," I said to Archie, who sat in the passenger seat, following my gaze, smearing the window with his wet nose. The tip of his tan-and-white tail twitched, a nascent wag. Why? In general, dogs are much less inscrutable than cats. They're as easy to read as a McDonald's menu. But this dog possessed motives that remained unsolvable, and here I was calling myself a detective. The unnerving, incessant staring, for one—what was that about? Dominance? He was going to establish it over me, by God, or die in the attempt? In the beginning, I was convinced he stared because I reminded him of a former owner, someone cruel and unrelentingly abusive who beat him every day with a rolled-up newspaper. We're products of our experience, even dogs; well, practically anything with a backbone. Maybe he felt the need to practice eternal vigilance or suffer another blow upside the head. The opposite could also have been true: I was the current in a long line of masters, each having abandoned him for any number of reasons, and this made it impossible for him to trust me, to bond with me, lest his canine heart be broken. It's hard to think of many things more psychologically shattering than abandonment. Rejection is like death without the mercy of death's finality. A little death, though the French called something else that.

So my idea was to spend more time with Arch, let him know I wasn't going anywhere. As with any relationship, you at least ought to act on the presumption you're in it for the long haul. The only things that stood in our way, in my mind, were the lease and that inexorable foe of all relationships, time.

"Well, the lights are on," I said. "She must be home."

I dialed the number. On the third ring, a man answered. I hung up. In less than a minute, my cell rang and her number popped up on the ID. I hit the talk button and almost said "Domino's Pizza." It was tempting.

"Someone just called from this number," the man said.

"That would be me."

"Who are you?"

"A friend of Katrina."

"Do you know where she is?"

"Well, that's why I called," I said. "I don't."

"Who is this?"

I took a deep breath. "Theodore Ruzak, Mr. Bates. I'm sitting in my car with my dog outside your house."

A shadow passed by a downstairs window.

"With your dog?"

"I've been trying to reach her all day. She won't answer her cell, and I'm a little worried about her, to be honest with you."

"I don't know where she is."

"She called me this afternoon around twelve-thirty, said she was on her way to meet me for lunch. She never showed."

A pause. Then: "Why was she meeting you for lunch?"

"I don't know."

"You don't know?"

"It wasn't clarified."

"Her idea?"

"One hundred percent."

"And the reason you're sitting outside my house with your dog?"

"Like I said. Worry."

Another pause.

"Why don't you come in, Mr. Ruzak."

"If it's okay with you."

"I extended the invitation."

"It's really none of my business," I said.

"No, it isn't. But come in anyway."

A chill went down my spine. In his picture, he reminded me of a vampire. Was I really prepared to go undaunted before the undead?

"Okay," I said. "I'll come."

"Leave the dog."

"He might bark," I said. "He may have abandonment issues."

"We have cats."

"Oh. Well, we could always talk on the portico."

"You don't like cats?"

"I'm allergic. Mildly. My concern lies more with the dog, those issues I just mentioned."

He acquiesced. "Then bring him. I'll shut the cats up."

He met us at the door, wearing a royal blue robe with matching slippers. If he had been holding a pipe, I would not have been surprised. He was taller than I expected, and lean, which made him appear even taller, with large hands, long, delicate fingers, dark eyes, and that aristocratic nose. Shoulder-length hair swept straight back from his alabaster forehead, streaked gray, slightly damp, as if I had caught him after his shower. He was stereotypically pale, like all vampires and most academics, with a look-right-through-you stare, a thinner, taller version of Bela Lugosi, able to dissect you right down to your spiritual marrow with a single, omniscient glance.

He creeped me out a little. Not Archie. He strained at his leash the moment Tom Bates opened the door; I had to yank him back to keep him from bowling him over. The tail went into overdrive, whipping back and forth into a tan-and-white blur. Tom Bates offered Archie his hand, palm down, and out came the tongue, kissing his fingertips.

"What's his name?"

"Archie."

"Friendly dog."

"Never met a stranger," I said, thinking, *Except his owner.* I extended my hand and he took it in his, fingers still wet with Archie's spit.

"Teddy Ruzak."

"I know."

"I guess you're Tom."

"You guess?" he asked.

"It's an expression."

"Really? Never heard that one. What's the context?"

"Usually when people meet for the first time."

"Ah."

"People also say, 'You must be,' like 'You must be Sam,' or 'You must be Alice.'" I felt like I was teaching a class for immigrants.

"Yes. Odd when you think about it."

"Most things are," I said. "When you think about them."

"Do you think that's the reason? Why most people don't?"

"I never thought about it."

He invited us inside. Inside was as impressive as outside. Gleaming hardwood floors, soaring twelve-foot ceilings, crown molding, antiques and original art in gilded frames, and I'm not talking about the kind you find at the Tomato Head. A house heavy with shadow, rich in echoes. The den I followed him into was decorated in a nautical theme. A ship's wheel hung on the wall behind his desk; model ships crowded the floor-to-ceiling bookshelves. The hardwood planks in this room were three inches wide and distressed, stained a molasses brown, like those found on the quarterdeck of a square-rigger. I thought of his family history and the fleet of vessels crossing the Atlantic, holds stuffed with human cargo.

He offered me a seat, which I accepted, and a drink, which I did not. I'd like to say Archie curled contentedly at my feet. That's what I'd like to say. He moved toward Tom as he took his position of command behind the desk, reached the end of his tether, and plopped down on his heinie, back toward me, nose lifted and working busily in Tom's direction, tail gently brushing the boards as he stared at him, I had no doubt, adoringly.

"So you haven't heard from her, either," I said.

"Not since last night."

"Have you notified the police?" I asked.

"Why would I notify the police?"

"She's missing."

He shook his head. "She's gone, Mr. Ruzak. Doesn't follow she's missing."

"'Gone'?"

"Purse, makeup, toiletries, some clothing, and her car. She's gone."

"Awful lot to take along for a lunch date."

He shrugged: *C'est la vie.*

"Maybe she changed her mind," he said. "About your date."

"She didn't leave a note or anything?"

"Neither a note nor anything else."

"And she won't answer your calls, either?"

"I don't know. I haven't tried."

"Why not?"

"Why would I? Katrina is a grown-up, Mr. Ruzak, and you, of course, know we haven't been having the best of times. We've separated."

"You moved out."

"I did."

"But you're here."

"And you'd like to know why."

"It's none of my business."

"No, it is not. But she'd be touched by your concern. I'll pass it along when we speak."

"Part of it's my fault," I said.

"Really?" He seemed bemused. "Which part?"

"The reason I'm checking up. I should clarify something. K.B. stands for Kinsey, not Katrina."

"Go on."

"I didn't want you to be confused."

"You've failed, then."

I tried again. "I didn't want you to think K.B. stood for Katrina Bates. It doesn't. It stands for Kinsey Brooks."

"Couldn't it stand for both?"

"Well, sure. I was talking about the file."

"What file?"

"The file you—" I stopped. He was looking at me with an expression of mild curiosity, like a collector in a gallery who has stumbled across an interesting piece by an obscure artist. *T. Ruzak, from his obfuscation period.*

"Okay," I said. "I get it. We can't talk about it. Well, just so you know."

"Just so I know . . . what?"

"The K.B. thing."

"Mr. Ruzak, have you been drinking?"

"I haven't even eaten."

"I didn't ask that."

"I never drink on an empty stomach."

"Then what is the explanation?"

"I just don't want anyone to go off half-cocked based on an erroneous interpretation."

"The assumption that simply because she's gone she must be missing?"

"Well, that, too."

"She's done it before. One might say it's been the leitmotiv of our marriage. Reach a rough spot, and Kat takes off to find a smoother one. One time, she left me and spent two weeks in Rome, hovering around the Vatican like a gypsy moth battering itself against a naked bulb. In the early years, she usually went to her parents' in the Hamptons."

"But she stopped?"

"One died and the other she doesn't talk to. Hasn't in nearly ten years."

"That's too bad, because when they're gone, they're, you know, gone."

"She'll come back. I give this latest juvenile ploy for attention a week, perhaps two. No more than three. She can't stand it, you see."

"Can't stand what?"

"Being away from me."

No smile. No ironical gleam in his eye. No expression at all in those black shark eyes set in a pale death mask. He wasn't joking. He was stating a fact: Katrina's love for him was as immutable as gravity.

"So, no, I haven't tried calling her. That's what she wants me to do. It's the point of running away. Women are manipulative, Mr. Ruzak."

"Not just women," I said.

"But no one uses it with more naked relish."

"Maybe my perceptions are shaped by my experience," I said.

"Aren't everyone's?"

"It just struck me as odd and a little disconcerting. She told me you were on your way here and she was on hers to the restaurant."

"When did she call?" he asked.

"About twelve-thirty."

"That would be right. I got here around twelve-forty-five."

"And she wasn't here."

"I wasn't expecting her to be. Last night she called and we arranged for me to pick up a few things. I would have been surprised if she were here."

"And you're not surprised she wasn't there? At the restaurant."

"As I've said, she must have changed her mind."

"Like she was going to meet me on her way out of town and decided not to."

"Yes."

"Is that in her character? I mean, to say 'I'll meet you there,' and then not without explaining why?"

"Our characters change with our circumstance, Mr. Ruzak. You're a PI and somewhat a student of human nature, yes?"

I nodded. The latter was truer than the former, and on both grounds I was shaky, but I nodded.

"Then you understand. Under normal circumstances, no, she wouldn't have stood you up."

"It's just that we spoke for some time and not once did she say anything about hitting the road."

"Why would she?"

"Because who am I?"

"Yes. Who are you?"

"Nobody really. You couldn't say friend and you could barely say acquaintance. She wasn't even my client anymore. The fact is, I hardly know Katrina at all."

He slipped into the opening I gave him and held forth on Katrina in a dry, professorial tone for about thirty minutes. It was a very long thirty minutes. Her upbringing (privileged, like his: nannies, exclusive schools, shopping trips to New York, London, Paris, a penthouse condo in Manhattan, homes in Connecticut and Southampton), her education (Dartmouth, then Harvard Law, where she graduated third in her class), her distant, eccentric father (who rarely addressed her by name, preferring to refer to her as "the girl," as if her gender diminished her in his eyes, and who was a notorious womanizer—when she was twelve, she caught him in bed with her eighteen-year-old nanny), her frail mother (who ignored her husband's infidelities at the expense of her physical and mental well-being, maintaining till her death the facade of the perfect aristocratic American family, even as the burden of her husband's liaisons, open secrets in the circles in which they traveled, slowly bore her down). Tom Bates must have considered himself, like a PI, somewhat a student of human nature, because after the vitae came the analysis of her character.

"She both hates and loves men, just as she both hated and loved her father, the first man in her life, the primal man, who was as distant with her as he was intimate with every other woman in his orbit, with the exception of Kat's mother, whom, according to Kat, he treated with total disdain. She turned a blind eye to his affairs, which, of course, made her utterly contemptuous. To Kat, too, understandably. Her mother enabled his addiction, and, just like every other addict, he resented the enabling even as he took full advantage of it."

"And then, of all people, she married you."

"Seeking to reconcile the irreconcilable? Reform the 'lost father'?" He was smiling. He didn't seem offended.

"She told me about your honeymoon. Feeling up the waitress."

"Totally innocent. I was brushing off some bread crumbs. But I understand your point, Mr. Ruzak. Our past is our destiny. It's probably no accident Kat married a man very much like her father and, I'm sure, a bitter irony to her that she woke up one day, only to discover herself in the very role she'd sworn she'd never play: the tired cliché of the long-suffering spouse to an unfaithful cad. She woke one day and found in the mirror her mother reborn."

"No wonder she wants to destroy you."

"Excuse me?"

My face got hot. I'd forgotten I'd taken that line out of the file before handing it over to Dresden Falks.

"I mean, I kind of got that impression from what you said, about loving and hating. One minute she was like, 'Get the bastard,' and the next it was all Tom this and Tom that. Comparing you to a Kennedy, kind of a cross between JFK and Russell Crowe in that gladiator movie. I can't remember the name of it. . . ."

"Gladiator," he said.

"He's this Roman general who gets set up by the emperor, sold into slavery, and then comes back as the greatest gladiator who ever lived."

"Gladiator," he said again.

"Right. A Roman gladiator. In ancient Rome."

"No, Mr. Ruzak, the name of the movie is *Gladiator.*"

"Well," I said. "That makes sense."

"Except, as I recall the plot, his character is a devoted family man."

"Right, even after they're brutally murdered. That hot Roman royal throws herself at him a couple of times and he says no."

"One wonders why Kat would compare me to him."

"Well, she didn't, not in so many words."

"Then why did you say she did?"

"I was reaching for a metaphor."

"And it slipped through your fingers."

"Wouldn't be the first time."

"I would say that *you* are more like Russell Crowe in this scenario, Mr. Ruzak."

"You would?" I was weirdly flattered.

"In the sense that your mission was to avenge the wrongs committed against an innocent."

"Except Katrina wasn't tortured, raped, and strung up like a slaughtered hog."

For the first time since we'd met, Tom Bates laughed.

"It's funny you say that, though," I went on. "I've been having this ongoing debate with my secretary about how I see my job. Not so much a gun for hire as a knight in shining armor."

"I like that, though you're a bit rotund for Quixote, with the dog you could pass for King Pellinore. And I suppose that would make me the Questing Beast."

"I've been meaning to bone up on my Arthurian legend, but Pellinore never catches the Questing Beast, right?"

"Precisely," he replied.

At that moment, something behind me caught his eye, and he waved his hand, crooking his index and middle fingers in an imperial gesture of command.

"It's fine; come on in," he called.

A luminous young woman stepped into the room, treading lightly on the weathered planks in her bare feet, as if she were afraid of getting a splinter. She was wrapped in a yellow towel, her hair wet as Venus's when the goddess emerged from the frothy surf.

"Kinsey, this is Mr. Theodore Ruzak."

"Hi," she said brightly. Then she swiveled away as gracefully as a ballerina on point, and said to Tom, "I'm making tea. Want some?"

"That would be lovely. Mr. Ruzak?"

"No thanks," I said. "It's getting late."

"Okay," she said in the same cheerful, slightly girlish voice. "Nice to meet you, Mr. Ruzzick."

She left. We watched her leave. The water dripping from her hair glistened on her exposed back. Tom Bates said, "A beautiful girl, like a beautiful poem, has the power to blow the top of your head off."

"Sometimes when my secretary comes into a room, I feel like

I'm expanding, or maybe like the room's shrinking. She's really pretty, too," I added, as if this was some kind of competition.

"Have you fucked her?"

"What?"

"Have you fucked her, or do you just lust after her?"

"Well," I said. The entire situation, like the Russell Crowe metaphor, had slipped completely through my fingers. "Neither one, really."

He gave a droll little chuckle.

"She has a live-in boyfriend," I said.

"And to fuck her would shatter the ideal of the chaste and honorable knight. Perhaps you're more Lancelot than Pellinore."

"I like Galahad," I said. "Going for the Grail."

"Do you like Kinsey?"

Huh? Staying up with this guy was like keeping pace with an Olympic sprinter.

"Um, sure. We just met, but I. . . . You bet."

"She's a bit young and inexperienced, but very open, very much in tune with her sexuality. It wouldn't take too much prodding."

What? What wouldn't take too much prodding? I shifted in my chair, clammy with nervous perspiration. I tended to dampen up when under duress.

"I really have to go," I said.

"So soon?"

"I just wanted to be sure," I said. "You know, she said she was coming and then she didn't, and she won't answer her phone, so I just wanted to be sure everything was okay."

"Everything is fine. If you like, I'll have her call you when she gets back."

"Well, that would be okay, I guess. Sure. If she doesn't mind."

"I think she'll be flattered. She understands I don't give a damn."

SCENE TWO
Litton's Diner

The Next Day

*A*t Litton's, you write your name and the number in your party on a chalkboard and wait to be called forward, like a kid to the front of the classroom, to be seated. I wasn't sure how that tradition started, but I suspected it had something to do with eliminating the need for a hostess. I wrote *Ruzak* and *2* on the board, then sat next to Felicia on the little bench under the poster of Neyland Stadium. Like the stadium, Litton's was a Knoxville landmark, sort of a mecca for burger lovers, in whose camp I happily resided.

"What an asshole," Felicia said. "How did she do it for twenty years? I couldn't have gone more than twenty minutes."

"When I was in high school, there was always the pretty, popular girl who fell for the doper."

"Savior complex," she said.

"'I can never say *how* I love.'"

"Who said that?"

"I don't remember."

"Let's make a new rule, Ruzak. From now on, you're not allowed to whip out a pithy quote unless you know who said it."

"What if I break it?" I had little confidence in my own self-control.

"A one-dollar fine."

"It's just that being original is so damn hard."

"A good PI talks less and listens more."

"Who said that?"

"I don't remember."

The waitress squinted at the board and called my name, or something roughly similar to it. I thought of Kinsey Brock and "Mr. Ruzzick." What was so tough about *Ruzak*? I almost mentioned this to Felicia but then thought better of it. I didn't want to hear "It's one of the few things about you that is."

I ordered a burger platter and a Coke. Felicia ordered a house salad and water.

"Are you a vegetarian?" I asked.

"No. Why?"

"Every time we go out, you order a salad."

"Maybe I'm trying to set an example."

"You can't eat at Litton's and not order a burger. It's like refusing to kiss the Pope's ring."

"I am," she said. "Besides the fact this perv wanted to pimp out his girlfriend, what's bugging you about him?"

"It's very easy to lie by word," I said. "A lot harder by deed."

"New rule, Ruzak: Who said that?"

"Me."

"Okay. Just checking."

"What he said makes sense. What he's doing doesn't. He moves back into the house the very day Katrina takes off, even brings his girlfriend with him."

"What's nonsensical about that?"

"For all he knows, any minute Katrina's going to walk through the front door and find them going hot and heavy on the hard-wood."

"A function of his arrogance. This is the guy who felt up the waitress on his honeymoon."

"What I mean is, it's like he *knows* she won't be coming home."

"Maybe he does and he doesn't think it's any of your damn business."

"That's the thing, I guess. It isn't."

"And not what we really need to talk about, Ruzak. You waste time on peripherals. What are we going to do about the Hinton problem?"

"You want to know why I sucked at baseball when I was a kid?"

She closed her eyes. A line appeared between her eyebrows. Maybe she had a headache.

"I don't know, Teddy. There are so many possibilities."

"I always closed my eyes right before I swung the bat."

"Okaaay," she said.

"We still have a little money in the bank. We could close up shop till I take the next exam."

"Let's face it, Ruzak," she said, eyes open again. "You're just a tad better at doing it than you are being tested on it."

"Throw in the towel? But then what would you do?"

"Why are you worried about me?"

"I meant to say 'we' or 'me.' It just came out as 'you.'"

She laughed. When Felicia laughed, a cute crinkle appeared on the bridge of her nose.

"Don't worry about me, Ruzak. I had a different shitty job before I took this one."

"It's that bad?"

Our food came. The burger was juicy, the fries were crisp and salty, and the plastic quart-size cup containing my soda was bottomless. Felicia dipped a quarter-size piece of lettuce into her dressing and sipped her water.

"What would you do if you couldn't be a detective anymore?" she asked.

"I'm not one now."

"You know what I meant."

"I don't know. Maybe go back to school. Well, I never actually went, so you couldn't characterize it as going back. Maybe something in anthropology or medicine."

"Dr. Ruzak?"

"It's a stretch," I admitted. "For a guy who can't pass something as simple as a PI exam."

"Maybe you could just hang around the med school and meet some nice brilliant grad."

"I can't picture myself as a kept man."

"So you've taken it that far," she said, smiling. "You've considered it."

"I'm not a moocher," I said, which wasn't precisely a denial. "My dad was in sales."

"Forget it, Ruzak. You'd make a terrible salesman. You're too honest."

"Tell that to Walter Hinton."

"You're honest where it counts."

"There're places where it doesn't?"

"I say you climb to the top of the highest ivory tower you can find and every ten years or so descend to impart your wisdom to the masses."

"It's better to be implacable than wise," I said. And this time, it was something *I* said.

SCENE THREE
Krispy Kreme Doughnut Shop

Eight Days Later

Dresden Falks watched the ladies in their white smocks and hair nets work their magic behind the plate glass separating the dining room from the vats and conveyor belts, where the glistening doughnuts rode. Falks was wearing a light summer sport coat over a Ralph Lauren button-up shirt and chinos. I was wearing an old Cardinals T-shirt, jeans, and doughnut droppings.

It was a little after 9:00 A.M., and the HOT sign was lighted.

"See that one in the middle?" he asked, raising his Styrofoam cup and extending his index finger in her direction. "Dead ringer for my elementary school cafeteria lady. Somewhere in America there must be a factory that churns them out, the big barrel-chested cafeteria slash food-assembly-line hair netter."

I sipped my coffee. For some time I had been having an internal debate over which shop brewed the best coffee, Krispy Kreme or Dunkin'. The other day, I had been startled to find Dunkin' Donuts coffee in the grocery store. Was that a measure of the superiority of its bean or an indication of its market share? Krispy

Kreme sold its coffee by the bag, too, but only in its stores. Since that day, I had been leaning toward Krispy Kreme, with the understanding that I had a soft spot for the underdog.

Falks ate the last of his second doughnut. He had ordered just two. I had four. I used to get two. Then I would troop back to the counter for a couple more, because two never quite did the trick. Eventually, I gave up and began ordering four to spare myself the embarrassment of a second trip to the counter.

"So how's that hottie secretary?" he asked. "What's her name, Felicity?"

"Felicia."

"Felicia. Felicia. Right."

"She lives with a firefighter."

"I know. You told me."

"I've never met him, but I hear he's a hothead."

"That's funny."

"No joke. He has a black belt and he knows how to use it."

"Okay. I thought maybe you were about to make a crack about the size of his hose."

It wasn't the same, grabbing a dozen at the drive-thru for the office or home. Little difference in taste, but eating inside when the sign was lighted was true and total immersion in the milieu of Kreme, down to and including the big women behind the big glass working the big conveyor belt; it was the difference between dipping your toe in and jumping into the deep end. When I left the shop, the smell would linger in my clothes, like a camper crawling into his sleeping bag reeking of wood smoke. I would depart all warm, sugary, and moist.

"You said there was something you wanted to discuss," I reminded him. He had been making small talk, waiting for me to bring it up, an annoyingly petty power play.

"Ran into a mutual acquaintance yesterday."

He paused: My cue to ask the obvious question, as if this were a play and he was the star/director.

"Guy by the name of Hinton," he finally said.

"He works for the state."

"Right. And he's got your ass in his crosshairs."

"He's dogged," I said.

"Said he shut you down last winter."

"He did."

"I got the impression he doesn't like you very much, Ted."

"He doesn't."

"Wanted to know what I know."

"Why would he think you would?"

"It's a close-knit profession, Ted. Only so much work in town; there's bound to be some overlap."

"Like the Bates case."

"Right, like that." He sipped his coffee and made a face. "Doughnuts are good, but the coffee sucks."

"It's better than Dunkin'," I said a bit defensively.

"No way. They even have it at Kroger now."

"What does that prove?"

"It proves they sell a hell of a lot of it."

"Maybe it proves they're desperate to shore up their profits because Krispy Kreme is kicking their butt."

"Why the anger, Ted? You a shareholder?"

"I'm not angry."

"It just strikes me as disproportionate. All I said was that the coffee sucks."

"Dres," I said. "I'm not an entirely idle guy. There are some things I need to take care of today."

"You're going through a hard time. I get it," he said. "And the times themselves aren't great. Gas prices, foreclosures, unemployment, inflation, war, you name it. Times like these, you gotta look after your own. That's what I told our buddy Wally Hinton. We're not cops, but we're not civilians, either, you know? Not the thin blue line, but a thin gray one, maybe. Like I would *ever* rat out a colleague."

"Well, I appreciate that, Dres. Though technically I'm not a colleague, but a competitor."

"My Dunkin' to your Krispy Kreme?"

I took a big bite of doughnut number three and chewed deliberately.

"Right."

"It's only a matter of time, you know. Sooner or later, he keeps turning over enough stones, he's gonna have what he needs to toss your ass in jail."

"I'm working on it."

"What, Ted? What are you working on?"

"Did Dunkin' consult Krispy Kreme before it shipped its coffee off to Kroger?"

"I'm Dunkin'. You're Krispy Kreme."

"I really appreciate your concern, Dres, but Hinton's my problem."

"You're out of step with the times, Ruzak. You're like a dentist handing out shots of whiskey while your competition dispenses the Novocain. This is the age of incorporation and takeover and monopolization. A solo operator just can't make it."

"Sounds like you're offering me a job," I said, hesitantly, though, because the notion seemed so utterly absurd. It sounded even crazier when I gave it voice.

"I don't got that kind of pull. But I could put in a kind word with the old man. He has a soft spot for the little guy. He started as a one-man shop, back in the Stone Age, just like you. Plus, I think he'd like you."

"How come?"

"You both got this Fred Flintstone kind of vibe going. Plus, you don't let yourself get bogged down in niceties."

"Niceties like selling you the Bates file."

"Right."

"Which could also demonstrate an unwillingness to get bogged down in niceties like loyalty and honesty."

"Heck, I'm not saying a corner office with Fridays off, Teddy. A foot in the door. That's all I'm saying. A foot in the door."

"And what about my secretary?"

"Hinton's gonna shut you down. She's losing her job one way or the other, Ted. Though she *is* fine, and the old man likes 'em pretty."

"What about the receptionist?"

"What receptionist?"

"At Velman. The reject from the ugly factory."

"Her? She's gone, man. Tossed her out on her fat ass after seeing yours. Not your fat ass; I mean your secretary's. Call it professional jealousy."

"Great. Now I feel responsible."

"Well, Ted, she wasn't fired over *your* looks."

"So you think Velman might hire both of us?"

"If that's your price, okay, a package deal."

"My price? My price for what?"

He lifted his cup to drink, but it was empty.

"See, as an employee of Velman, you won't need a license to be a dick. The company holds the license and you hold your dickiness."

"Where is Katrina Bates?" I asked.

He pivoted neatly with me. "Savannah."

"Savannah, Georgia?"

"There another Savannah?"

"How do you know?"

"She told my client."

"Your client felt the need to share that with you?"

"We're anticipating a very nasty divorce case, Ruzak, involving lots of embarrassing details and lots and lots and lots of money. It's a need-to-know thing."

"So you've verified it."

"Why would he lie about it?"

"What's in Savannah?"

"Never been, but I hear a nice beach, a college, and I think it's where they filmed that movie about the retarded guy who kept running into presidents."

"No, I meant why would she go there?"

"What is this, Ruzak? You got feelings for her?"

"Just a generic bad one. I sell you my client's confidential case file and a few days later my client disappears."

"But she didn't disappear. She's in Savannah."

"According to the estranged husband with lots of embarrassing details and lots and lots and lots of money to lose."

"Right." He laughed, for some reason. "Well, you could always head on down there and check it out, I guess. Why you would, I can't figure."

"I have a bad feeling," I said. "Like I said."

"Bad feeling," he echoed. "Bad feelings are worthless, Ruzak. Bad feelings are for teenagers jacking off and papists waiting in line at the confessional. Our business is facts."

I shifted uncomfortably in my chair. It felt like I was already on board, Dresden Falks's newest trainee.

"Well, that's what my feeling is. A fact."

SCENE FOUR
Lobby of the Sterchi Building

Four Days Later

*W*hittaker fairly leapt at me from his hiding place behind one of the columns, at the midway point of my third trek from the elevators to the front doors. I would have offered my hand, but it was full, like the other one, with Archie's crate. The crate (you never call it a cage, though that is precisely what it resembled) was designed to be easily broken down for convenient storage or travel. I, however, had never quite gotten the hang of it. Fortunately, fully assembled, it fit, albeit snugly, in the backseat of my Sentra.

"Mr. Ruzak, does this mean what I think it means?"

"It just might."

"You've found a home for Archie."

"How do you know his name?"

His mouth came open. No sound came out.

"You were snooping around my apartment, weren't you?" I asked.

"Of course not. You must have told me."

"I don't remember telling you."

"The dog's name is not the point, Mr. Ruzak."

"No, it's how you got it."

"No, it's if you're finally going to comply with your lease."

"Mr.—" I began, then took a breath, then said, because I still wasn't sure which it was, first name or last, "Look, Whittaker, I could stand here and bandy words with you all day—"

"'Bandy'? Who does that? Who uses words like *bandy*?"

"At least one person," I said. "Can I finish my thought? I'm running late."

"Yes or no, Mr. Ruzak, are you discarding the dog?"

"Yes, I am casting off the canine."

He gave me a hard, appraising stare, looking right into my eyes, as if he were counting blinks, the poor man's lie detector.

"Are we done?" I asked. "They're waiting on me and this is kind of heavy."

"We reserve the right to monitor your compliance," he said archly.

"Oh, I'm done with the whole pet thing," I assured him. "I've discovered Second Life." On impulse, I shoved the crate into his chest. He brought his arms up instinctively. "Hold this a sec for me, will ya, while I run up and get the dog? Thanks."

When I returned, the crate was on the floor by the lobby doors, Whittaker standing beside it in the same suit he always wore, or something nearly identical to it, and I wondered where his money went, because it couldn't be for clothes. Archie yanked on his leash at the sight of him, and I thought of my father, the guy who never met a stranger, the guy who was often kinder to strangers than to his own family, even to his only son, the bearer of his name and legacy, toward whom the attitude more often than not resembled a shopper with buyer's remorse.

Archie ducked his head under Whittaker's hand for a stolen caress. Incredibly, Whittaker complied.

"Maybe you'd like to adopt him," I said.

"You said you already found a home." Smug.

"I said I was getting rid of him. Maybe I'm taking him back to the pound."

"Are you taking him back to the pound?"

"Maybe you've given me no choice."

"You signed the lease, Mr. Ruzak."

"This should teach me," I said. "I was just trying to do some good."

"Your misplaced philanthropy is not my responsibility."

"We all have to do our part. We can't save the world, but we can help whatever little wayward satellite that comes into our orbit."

"You're saying I should take this dog." He actually seemed to be considering it. Archie was licking his fingertips and Whittaker was letting him.

"Are you saying you would?"

"Of course not!"

"Might?"

"It's a moot point now."

"Let me ask you something. When you break into my apartment—"

"I do not break into your apartment, Mr. Ruzak."

"When you gain entrance to my apartment, you let Archie out of his crate, don't you? Play with him, give him a treat, maybe."

"That's outrageous."

"He seems to know you pretty well, that's all."

"I don't deny he must recognize me."

He pulled his hand away and Archie doggedly pursued it, trying to push his wide, flat head underneath it. Whittaker shoved both hands into his pockets.

"You've fallen in love with my damn dog," I said.

"I don't give a damn about your damn dog."

"The feeling isn't mutual."

"What are you trying to do, Ruzak? What do you want? I'm not heartless. I don't want anything bad to happen to this animal. I'm not the one who chose to adopt it and house it in a pet-free facility. I'm not the one who locks it up in a cage for eight, nine hours a day with no companionship and no exercise. That's the irony here. You're lucky I didn't call the ASPCA on you."

"It's called a crate, and I don't lock it up the whole time. Just the other day, he went with me on a case."

"On a case?"

"I'm a PI."

"You're kidding."

"In fact, this dog has been beneficial to my work."

"What, like Scooby-Doo?" Sarcastic.

"Well, given that scenario, you might be a bad guy. All the bad guys were caretakers, janitors, and property managers."

"And his Shaggy has a thyroid problem." Caustic.

Archie sat at his feet and lifted one paw. I watched, astounded. Where had he picked that up? When Whittaker ignored the offered paw, Archie waved it urgently at him.

"Look," I said. "He's waving good-bye."

"You and this dog get the hell out of my building, Ruzak."

SCENE FIVE
Felicia's House

Forty-five Minutes Later

She met us at the door wearing black jogging shorts and a tight white T-shirt that reminded me of that soccer player's sports bra, the one bared to the world when the U.S. women's team took the World Cup a few years back. She had pulled her blond hair into a ponytail, the ends of which were still damp, and a drop or two of moisture clung to the exposed skin between her shoulder blades. I thought of Kinsey Brock, fresh from her shower, and the yellow towel and the way a woman's wet skin looks in ambient light, and suddenly my heart felt burdened, and I became unnaturally aware of my tongue, an appendage you don't normally pay that much attention to, but which now seemed swollen and hypersensitive, too large by half for my mouth.

"I didn't know you jogged," I said.

"I don't," she replied. She called for her kid, Tommy, and I heard a loud bumping and banging down the hall, as if a barricade were being torn down. I hung on to the end of Archie's leash like a ship lashed to a buoy lest it be dragged out to sea.

"Was that Bob's truck in the drive?" I asked.

"Of course. Ruzak, you know I don't own a truck."

"Finally I get to meet him."

"He's asleep. He's been flipped to the night shift."

"I thought firefighters slept at the station."

"It's not a prison, Teddy. They do let you go home once in awhile."

Tommy barreled into the room, sliding on his knees the final two feet, straight into Archie's chest. The reunion could only be characterized as joyful, lots of screaming (Tommy), licking (Archie), and roughhousing (both), Archie scampering after the kid in mock retreat, forelegs stiff, entire rear end in motion, which gave that old saw about the dog-wagging tail some credence.

"Tell me why you're going to Savannah again?" Felicia asked. She was drinking a vitamin water. Maybe there was a treadmill somewhere. Or she was fresh from the gym. I had never given much thought to how she kept her shape; I just appreciated it.

"I have a bad feeling."

She sniffed. "You and your feelings."

She wasn't wearing any makeup. A fine spray of freckles dotted her nose and cheeks. Beads of perspiration clung above her upper lip. *That little cleft right underneath our noses is called the philtrum,* I reminded myself. *Christ, Ruzak, what the hell does that matter?* Sometimes when I was around Felicia, I lost a bit of mental discipline, long-dormant neurons containing information like what a philtrum is suddenly firing, threatening to overwhelm my cerebral cortex.

"What's so wrong with intuition?" I asked. "Some of the greatest crimes in history were cracked on a hunch."

"Name two."

"I should confess part of it is to alleviate my own sense of responsibility."

"Which is totally misplaced. Her taking off had nothing to do with you, Ruzak."

"Unless the facts bear out my bad feeling."

"'K.B. having illicit liaison with BF'?"

"Here's the hypothetical—"

"Great. The hypothetical. Wait, let me sit down first. Tommy, honey, why don't you take Arch outside and throw the ball?"

"What ball?" Tommy barked. He tended to bark everything.

"The old tennis ball. It's in the azaleas, next to the fence."

Tommy ran to the sliding glass door. Archie needed no urging. The family room seemed uncomfortably quiet after they slammed outside, like a movie theater before the show starts and you're the only person in the place.

"You play tennis?" I asked.

"No." She flopped onto the sofa and drew her bare legs tightly against her black-clad bottom. On the coffee table in front of her was a stack of papers and a yellow highlighter. She reached over— her bare arm seemed incredibly long—and flipped the papers over. The highlighter rolled off the table. She picked it up and placed it on top of the papers. "Now. Hypo."

"Tom's worried about the file. He buys it from me, through Dresden Falks, finds out K.B. is having an affair with BF."

"And he thinks K.B. is Katrina."

"Right."

"Jealous rage."

"Yes."

"Calls Katrina. Says he needs to pick up a few things."

"Right."

"Katrina calls you, invites herself to lunch."

"At twelve-thirty-six."

"Twelve-thirty-six? That's precise."

"It's on my caller list."

"But Tom shows up before she can get out the door."

"Yes."

"Big fight. 'Who is BF?'"

"Or he thinks he knows who."

"Doesn't matter."

"Right."

"He picks up the nearest deadly weapon. Knife, revolver, candlestick, lead pipe, what have you. No more cheating K.B."

"Then he cleans it up, grabs some of her clothes, a suitcase maybe, purse, makeup, throws it all—and her—into her car and, I don't know, pushes it off Lake Loudon pier. No big deal. She's taken off in the past. They're breaking up, not unusual for someone to have a freak-out and take off."

"Then you show up and catch him and his little girlfriend post-coitus."

"That's an assumption."

"Ruzak, the whole goddamned thing is an assumption."

"Well."

"'Where's Katrina?' our hypothetical gumshoe asks."

"I'm not hypothetical," I protested.

"You're not a gumshoe, either. Tom lays it on thick, throws in the offer of bedding his paramour as a sort of goodwill gesture, so you'll think what a terrific guy Tom Bates is."

"It was creepy," I admitted. "'Prodding.' The imagery."

She laughed, for some reason. Felicia, like a lot of women her age, actually looked younger without makeup.

"Later, though, Tom starts to get a little worried. What if this oversized wanna-be starts nosing around his cover? So he dispatches his lackey Dresden Falks to make a little quid pro quo over doughnuts. Sort of like Darth Vader offering the galaxy to Luke in the first movie."

"That was the second movie."

"Right, and it wasn't over doughnuts and Dres didn't cut off your hand with a light saber, so let's throw out the whole hypothetical."

"The facts fit. Mostly."

"One fact doesn't. Boba Fett Falks told you where she was. Not that they had no clue where she was. Not that she *might be* there, but that she *was* there."

"And that means . . . What does that mean?"

"Plus, it isn't Seattle. Tom told you she's flown all the way to Rome before, but it's not Rome, either. Not Rome or Greece or Australia, but Savannah, Georgia. A little town only a few hours' drive away."

"Easy to confirm."

"A terribly stupid lie from a terribly smart man."

"Therefore it's not a lie. She really is in Savannah. But I called every hotel and bed-and-breakfast and real estate agency in town and there's no record of her."

"So she's staying with friends. That would be the most logical scenario. She's going through a really bad time, maybe the worst time in her life, and she's got to turn to someone for support."

"I'm wasting my gas." I didn't say "time." These days, gas is more precious.

"Let's say you're able to prove the negative. She isn't in Savannah. That she's dead doesn't follow. Maybe she left. Maybe by the time you get there, she will be on a flight to Australia."

"But I might find her."

"And then what?"

"And then my bad feeling goes away."

"It *is* about you, isn't it, Ruzak?"

"That's what this was all about, wasn't it?" I asked, meaning the hypo walk-through. "Getting me to see that."

"You already saw it. It's okay, you know. It might even be good for you to get out of town for a few days, but come back, Ruzak. Knoxville wouldn't be the same without you."

She walked me to the door. She didn't smell sweaty. She smelled like peaches.

"Maybe if I find her, I'll feel differently about Falks's offer."

"Can you see yourself working for a place like Velman? I can't."

"There'd be benefits," I said. "Insurance. Paid vacations. Maybe even a retirement fund."

"Velman needs the competition. It's why they broke up the phone company, Ruzak."

"Thanks," I told her. "For keeping Archie."

"My rates are very reasonable."

She was standing very close to me. I didn't think it was on purpose—the entryway was tiny. But her face was lifted up toward mine (I was a good foot taller than she was) and without her wearing makeup, I could see the fine hairs in the folds of her philtrum, and her lips were parted slightly and there was the tip of her tongue, pink and glistening, and my heart nearly collapsed under its burden. There is no longing that does not eventually lead to regret; Bob was asleep in the bedroom just down the hall and so what I coveted could be stolen, but I was no Tom Bates. If I closed the gap, if I smashed my mouth into hers, I would tear out the rivets holding the universe together. It was like the monkeys: You can yank them from their habitat, throw a diaper on them, and stick them in a high chair and take them to parks to ride the teeter-totter, but still the day comes when the beast goes for your jugular with his two-inch canines. I wasn't that monkey in a diaper and I wasn't Tom Bates and, most important, I wasn't firefighter Bob. I was Ruzak.

SCENE SIX
Tybee Island, Georgia

The Next Day

I parked in the driveway of the beach cottage on Center Terrace, a few feet behind the silver Mercedes convertible, and dialed Felicia's cell number.

"Are you at the office?" I asked her.

"Yes."

I could hear a cartoon show blaring in the background. About a year ago, Felicia had brought in a television to keep Tommy entertained on those days when he had nowhere else to go. It had seemed a good compromise at the time, a way to keep Felicia in the office when the baby-sitting arrangements fell through, which seemed to happen a lot. The difficulty lay with discussing a client's problem while the Cartoon Network blasted in the next room and the prints rattled on the walls.

"I need you to pull a tag for me," I said.

"You found her car."

"Maybe. It's a Tennessee tag. Foxtrot-Xiphophyllus-Yellow space Lion-David-Yellow."

"Xiphophyllus?"

"It's a kind of leaf."

"You could have said Xerox or xylophone."

"Xiphophyllus was the first word that came to mind."

"A leaf?"

"Mom was an avid gardener."

"So it's FXY space LDY?"

"Right."

"Foxy Lady?"

"It's a vanity plate."

"Classy. Hang on."

"Call me back," I said.

I cut the engine and stepped out into the monochrome atmosphere: The sky was a solid sheet of gray, the rain a foggy, enveloping mist, making me regret leaving my hat and umbrella at home. The Mercedes was parked underneath the cottage, between the pylons upon which the structure rested, raised high in the event of a storm surge. The car doors were locked. The engine was cold. There were stairs leading to the wraparound porch up top. From there you could see the deserted beach with sand the color of piecrust and the Atlantic, its gray only slightly darker than the sky's, the horizon disconcertingly missing as gray faded into gray. I knocked on the door and waited. On impulse, I hit the speed-dial button for Katrina Bates's cell phone. The call went straight to her voice mail. I hung up. Two seconds later, my cell rang.

"Bingo," Felicia said. "Silver 2007 Mercedes SL, registered to Thomas and Katrina Bates. Where'd you find it?"

"At their beach house."

"Beach house?"

"I checked with the property-tax office."

"I'm impressed. Are you on your way home?"

"I'm here. At the house."

"Let me guess. Nobody's home."

"Nobody's answered the door yet."

"Can you see inside?"

"No. Blinds are drawn. I'm walking around to the front."

White rocking chairs faced the sea, the kind with the oversized arms, just right for resting your coffee cup while you contemplated the restless tides, the eternal comings and goings. By this point, my hair was plastered to my head and cold droplets clung to my eyebrows. I shivered. The elements don't give you a cold; germs do. I told myself that, and then I sneezed.

"Nope," I said. "Can't see in here, either. That was a side door. I'll knock on this one."

"Just because she isn't there doesn't mean she isn't *there*," Felicia said.

"See if you can find a listing for this house," I said. "Probably under their name, but let me give you the address." I recited it.

"Hang on."

"Call me back."

I sank into one of the rockers and immediately felt water soak into my khakis. This was one of the things that made me such a terrific detective, my keen skills of observation. I was no coastal dweller, but it appeared the tide was out. The surf seemed muted, almost sullen, like the rain. A necklace of raindrops clung to the whitewashed railing, quivering, not quite heavy enough to fall. My cell rang.

"It's under his name," she said. "Unlisted. What are you doing, Ruzak?"

"Sitting in a rocking chair in my wet underwear."

"You went for a dip?"

"It's raining," I said. "And I never go in the ocean."

"Can't swim?"

"Too many creatures. If she isn't here, why is her car?"

"She's taking a walk."

"Horrible day for that."

"Some people like to. Maybe she walked to town."

"Savannah is twenty miles away."

"Or over to a friend's house."

"That's something I could check out."

"Can you explain, after he told you where she was and you found her car there, why you actually need to lay your hands on her?"

"I'd settle for just my eyes." Which I now proceeded to rub. I hadn't slept much the night before. I never did in hotels. "Any calls?"

"No, but Walter Hinton came by this morning, looking for you. Your great-aunt died, in case he asks."

"My great-aunt?"

"Her name is Regina. Regina Ruzak."

"It's a little obvious," I said. "Too alliterative."

"What do you want from me, Ruzak? I had to think fast."

"Did he say what he wanted?"

"Your files. I told him the usual charge for one file was twenty thousand dollars but that we had a special this week: Buy one, get the second one half price. He said he was coming back with a search warrant."

"You know something? As crimes go, I had no idea practicing detection without a license was so serious."

"He's got a vendetta against you."

"I don't think it's that," I said. "When you get something caught in your eye, you just want the pain in your eye to stop."

She said, "Huh?"

"It doesn't matter whether it's an eyelash or a grain of sand. It's hurting your eye. It about your eye."

"Back when I was a card-carrying member of the mean-girl clique in middle school, we would eyeball people's heads between our thumbs and index fingers and pretend to squish them. Squish their heads. That's what I want to do now, Ruzak. Squish your head."

"You and Walter Hinton."

"He represents a pressing concern *here* that you're being *there* isn't going to help. He's the sty in *your* eye, Ruzak."

I returned to my car and sat for a minute staring at FXY LDY. Developing a rash from the moisture, my butt began to itch. A quick canvass of the neighborhood, then back to the hotel for a warm shower and to check out. The window of opportunity to pack up the files before Hinton returned with his warrant was narrowing. I noticed a sign hanging on a waist-high wooden pole at the end of the driveway. "FOR RENT," it said, with a phone number beneath the words. I dialed the number.

"Tybee Island Rentals," a woman answered in a rich Low Country drawl.

I told her I was interested in one of their properties and gave her the address.

"Is it available?" I asked.

"When would you like it?"

"Tonight."

"How many days?"

"One. Just one. Just tonight."

"I'm sorry, sir. There's a one-week minimum for that property."

"Okay. This week. Beginning tonight."

"Can you hold? I have to check." After a minute that seemed much longer than a minute, she came back on. "You're in luck."

"Are you sure?" I asked. "I just drove by and there's a car in the drive."

"I'll double-check. . . . No, it should be empty. Are we talking about the same house? We manage several rentals on Tybee."

"Pretty sure," I said. "Huh. Maybe I got it wrong."

"Would you like to reserve it? I can hold it with a credit card."

I started the car and backed onto Center Terrace.

"Where's your office?" I asked. "I'm on my way now."

SCENE SEVEN
Tybee Island Rentals

Minutes Later

*H*er name was Melody Moy, and she was the owner of the smoky Low Country drawl. A natural blonde pushing forty, I guessed, who knew her assets and how to leverage them: Her white blouse was just a bit too tight and her skirt just a bit too short, the paint on her nails and the rouge on her cheeks just a bit too red. She had the paperwork on her desk when I walked through the door. The rental agreement was six single-spaced pages long and filled with boilerplate. I felt like I was making a major purchase.

"And how much for the week?" I asked her.

"Two thousand."

"Whew. I'm going to invest in rental property," I said. She laughed, like she had never heard that one before. When she laughed, I noted a crinkle developed on the bridge of her nose.

"Are you in town for business or pleasure, Mr. Ruzak?"

"Neither," I said. "My great-aunt died. Auntie Regina. She retired down here about twenty years ago."

"Oh, I'm so sorry."

"We weren't very close, but there's a will."

"Oh, and you're thinking of investing in property." I could tell she felt bad for having laughed earlier.

"No, I was making a joke," I said. "The truth is, I planned on staying just a couple of days—the funeral's tomorrow—but after walking on the beach, I thought I should seize this opportunity to take a break."

"We all need that," she said. "I haven't had a real vacation in five years."

"I'm a workaholic, too," I said.

"Oh, I'm not *holic* in anything," she said with a laugh. She had a good laugh, not giggly and not originating too deep in her belly. "It's not a matter of *won't,* but *can't.*"

"You own the business?"

"My husband started it. We divorced. I got it."

"That's the way it is," I said. "Not divorce. I meant when you're running your own shop. Never a day off."

"Are you speaking from experience, Mr. Ruzak?"

"I'm a consultant."

"That's usually code for 'unemployed.'"

"Just the opposite. I need some time off. I'm stretched thin." Immediately, I regretted the word: It might draw attention to the fact that I wasn't. I had my checkbook but gave her the company credit card instead. After the unemployed remark, I was afraid she might refuse to take a check.

"'The RAG'?" she said, looking at the card.

"The Research & Analysis Group. My company."

"Investment counseling?"

"Um."

We both held our breath while her device contacted the bank to verify my solvency. She ripped off the register tape, I signed, and

she dug into her desk for the key. She sighed, shook her head—
a swirl of blondness followed by a whiff of White Diamonds—
pushed back from the desk, rose, walked over to the filing cabinet,
opened the bottom drawer, and bent from the waist to fish in the
contents. The hem of her skirt drew up two inches. Her legs were
bare and the same color as the sand on Tybee Island. My stomach
growled.

SCENE EIGHT
The Cottage

A Few Hours Later

Night did not so much fall on the island as slam down, from gloomy to utter black in a matter of minutes. Accustomed to streetlamps and the clatter and beep of rail yards and traffic, I found this smack-down of darkness disconcerting, like a man with vertigo standing at the lip of the Grand Canyon. The rain whispered against the windows and the surf crashed beyond in muffled harmony. I turned on every light in the cottage, but nothing illuminating was illuminated: beds made, cupboards bare, closets and trash cans empty—even the refrigerator, and I was hungry. I resisted as long as I could—it felt a bit like checking in with Mommy—but I gave in around nine and called Felicia. She answered on the twelfth ring. Not that I counted.

"You're home," she said.

"Well," I said.

"You're on your *way* home."

"Um."

"You're still in Savannah."

"I'm on Tybee Island. In the Bates's getaway house."

"You broke into their house? Christ, Ruzak!"

"No, no. I rented their house."

I could hear her breathing. It was short, ragged breathing. She must have had to run for the phone. Then I heard a man's voice murmuring indistinguishably in the background.

"I'm interrupting," I said.

"Stop that."

"I'll hang up."

"Not you. Hey, please stop that. It's Ruzak . . . *Ruzak*. Go get me something to drink. . . . No, I want water. Are you there?"

"Me?"

"Sorry. Bob's off tonight."

"I'll let you go."

"Wait. Did you say you rented the house?"

"I wanted to get a look inside."

"Why?"

"To see what was inside."

"And?"

"Nothing. Clean as a model home. I don't think she's been here."

"Which proves?"

"Puzzling. Her car's here; she isn't."

"We're on the border of hypo territory, aren't we?"

"She got here, but never *got* here, maybe."

"Somebody snatched her?"

"The problem with that is she would have told Melody."

"Ah, Melody, of course. Who the hell is Melody?"

"The rental agent who manages the cottage for them. I told her about the car and she checked with Tom to make sure the place was available."

"And it is. Did she ask him about the car?"

"I don't know."

"Did *you* ask him about the car?"

"Why would I ask him about the car?"

"They have three, you know."

"I didn't. How do you?"

"I looked them up for you, remember? A Mercedes, a Jag, and a Hummer."

"A Hummer? That's irresponsible."

"Right, another strike against the bastard. Did Tom tell you which car was missing?"

"No."

"Maybe she drives the Jag in Knoxville and they leave the Mercedes at the beach house."

"Why?"

"So they have a car at the beach house. Thanks."

"For what?"

"Not you. My water. Did you talk to the neighbors?"

"I will tomorrow. Check around at some of the local hangouts."

"What about the car? Did you check around it?"

"It's locked. The windows are tinted, but it looks clean as a whistle, inside and out, like it's been detailed recently."

"Aha. You know what that means."

"What?"

"That car's been detailed recently. Would you please stop it? I'm sorry."

"It's okay."

"I wasn't apologizing to you. Look, give me five minutes, okay?"

"Okay."

"Not you."

Why didn't she cover the mouthpiece when she talked to him? I wondered how she had missed that lesson in basic phone etiquette.

"Why would they leave a very expensive car hundreds of miles away, in a place frequented by strangers?" I asked. "And why would they need two cars when they come down?"

"Maybe they fly down."

"Are there flights from Knoxville to Savannah?"

"I don't know. Maybe you should check that out."

"Why?"

"Good question. But I'm the dummy who can't figure out why you rented that house in the first place. Christ, would you please cut it *out?*"

"I've caught you at a bad time."

"Actually, it was pretty good." She giggled. I had never heard Felicia giggle. I felt voyeuristic, as invasive as peeking in her window while she changed. "Sit down. Sit down and stop that."

"You're breaking up pretty bad," I said, lying. "Maybe it's the rain. It's raining here. And dark. Damn dark. Dark and rainy."

"You're clear as a bell." I heard a slapping sound. I assumed it was her slapping him. Maybe it was a product of his profession, a profound, pervasive sense of urgency: *Fire, fire, fire, let's go!*

"You just won't stop, will you?" she asked. Who was she asking?

"Not you."

"I didn't say anything."

"Not you—Bob. I was talking to Bob."

"I'll let you do that."

"No, wait. You won't stop, either. What's this about, Ruzak? Every time there's a choice between an innocent explanation and an ominous one, you opt for the ominous."

"Maybe it's a product of my profession," I said. "This profound, pervasive sense of—"

"It's like you *want* something to be wrong."

"There's no such thing as a selfless act? This is part of my savior complex, the knight-in-shining-armor thing?"

"Exactly. What are you drinking?"

"Nothing."

"Not you."

"I know that."

"Let me have a sip," she said.

"Not me," I said.

"What?"

"The thing I know: not me. Not me."

I called Tom Bates's home number. A wispy little-girl voice answered. I asked to speak to Tom. What had Bob been drinking? Not beer: Felicia was a wine drinker; she never would have asked for a sip of beer. When you think of firefighters and alcohol, you think of beer. What self-respecting firefighter pranced about with a glass of Chardonnay? For most of my adult life, I had been sequestered as a security guard on night shift, my contact with fellow humans limited, and in that empty experiential space, stereotypes had flourished, difficult now to exorcize. For all I knew, 89 percent of all firefighters belonged to the wine-of-the-month club.

"Hello," Tom Bates said in a voice thick with sleep or too much Chardonnay, or maybe I was intruding upon yet another romantic interlude.

"This is Teddy Ruzak," I said. "You know."

"Yes."

"I forgot to ask you something the other night."

"Of course."

Did he mean "Of course, ask away," or did he mean "Of course, you would forget, you moron"?

"Which car does Katrina drive?"

"Which car? She usually drives the Jag."

"So the Jag is missing."

"No, I didn't say that. The Mercedes is missing. Or was. I understand it's been found."

"It's at the beach house," I said.

"You found it." It wasn't a question.

"A mutual friend told me she might be here."

"And is she?"

"Apparently not."

"That's odd."

"What I thought," I said. "What would possess her to drive down here, park the car, and then take off without it?"

"Something only Katrina could answer."

"What, like it's a dodge?"

"Is there anything else, Mr. Ruzak? I'm right in the middle of something."

I bet you are. "You haven't heard from her, then?"

"Nothing. Not a word."

"While I was in town, I thought I might ask around. Anybody she's particularly close to in Savannah?"

"No one she would confide in. We haven't used that house in almost two years, Mr. Ruzak."

"Can I ask you one more question? I'm sorry. I sometimes get these things stuck in my craw and it's the devil to get them out. I hate to put you on the spot."

"It's hard to imagine a scenario in which you could."

"Right. My question is about the future. Say you never hear from her again—"

He didn't wait for me to finish. He didn't need to. He must have already thought it through.

"I would probably have her declared legally dead. Life goes on, Mr. Ruzak."

"Unless you're legally dead."

"Or illegally. But it won't come to that. She'll be in touch."

"How do you know?"

"She always has in the past. Enjoy your stay in Tybee, Mr. Ruzak. If you're fond of Low Country cuisine, may I suggest the Crab Shack? The shrimp boil is excellent."

I wished he hadn't brought up food. I was looking up Pizza Hut's number when a banging commenced on the door. Why had I left my gun in Knoxville? If Felicia had been there, I would have pointed out that my leaving it was evidence of my congenital optimism: If I'd really suspected foul play, wouldn't I have brought the gun? I hadn't brought it, so I grabbed an iron skillet from the cupboard and called through the door, "Who is it?"

"It's me," Melody Moy called back. "Melody Moy!"

I opened the door and there she stood, cradling a bottle of Chardonnay and a cheese and fruit basket with the price tag still attached to the handle.

"All right if I come in?" she asked.

She stepped inside and I closed the door, which brought my face very close to her hair. She smelled of perfume and rain.

"What are you cooking?" she asked.

"I'm not," I said.

"You normally walk around with an iron skillet in your hand?"

"I thought you might be an intruder," I confessed.

"Intruders don't usually knock, do they?"

"It would be overly polite," I admitted.

"Not to mention counterproductive." She smiled, and her nose crinkled in the middle. "Have you already eaten?"

"I was just about to call for some delivery."

"Like an appetizer first?"

She set the basket on the coffee table and went into the kitchen, a bit wobbly on her heels on the thick pile until she reached the linoleum, where the stems made little dimples in the floor. She stuck the bottle in the freezer to cool.

"Hey," I said. "You didn't have to."

"I know," she said, falling onto the sofa and kicking off her shoes. Her toenails were painted the same bright bloodred hue as her fingernails. "But I'm an old-time southern girl, Mr. Ruzak. A death in the family calls for a potluck. Only I couldn't cook a green bean casserole if you paid me a thousand dollars."

"Your price is two thousand?"

She laughed that very good laugh. "You're funny. Actually, for a thousand bucks I'd boil a whole horse."

"You must not like horses."

"I *love* horses. I used to own one."

"What happened?"

"I got divorced. I got the business and the house; my husband got the horse."

"Not a bad trade."

"I don't know. I loved that horse."

"You could have filed for joint custody."

"Are you a lawyer, Mr. Ruzak? You talk like one."

"No," I said. I was at once flattered and ashamed. "I'm a consultant."

"That's right. The RAG. Are you going to put that pan down and have a seat? You're making me nervous."

I put the pan next to the basket, then hesitated on where to put myself. She had flopped onto the middle cushion, narrowing my options. The nearest chair seemed too far away; sitting in it might be interpreted as a transparent act of rejection. As a compromise, I sank onto the ottoman next to the coffee table.

"Are you married, Teddy? Do you mind if I call you Teddy?"

"No, to both."

"Been married?"

I shook my head no.

"Well, that's a stumper. Someone attractive as you. You must be homosexual."

"No, I'm straight. I guess I haven't found the right girl."

She smiled. Her lips glistened. I pictured her sitting in her car before coming up, reapplying her lipstick in the rearview mirror.

"Definition, please," she said.

"Oh, I've never gone that far. It's one of those things like pornography."

"Excuse me? Like . . . pornography?"

"I'll know her when I see her."

"You just haven't seen her."

"Not yet."

"I don't believe you," she said. "How old are you?"

"Thirty-four."

"A man doesn't reach the age of thirty-four without falling in love at least once."

"I was engaged, years ago. She broke it off when she decided I didn't have a future."

"And now she would cry in her soup."

"Oh, I'm not the vindictive type. I wished her the best. Still do."

"But the torch burns brightly still."

I didn't say anything. My eyes slid from her glistening lips to her bare legs, stretched straight out and crossed at the ankles. There was a tattoo of a blue-winged butterfly on the left one.

"Too personal. I'm sorry," she said.

"It was a long time ago. Hey, thanks for bringing the basket and the wine. That was really thoughtful."

I shot up from the ottoman and went to the kitchen for the wine. I found two glasses above the sink but couldn't find the opener. She watched me from the sofa as I opened and closed drawers.

"Look in the bucket," she called.

"What bucket?"

"The bucket by the fridge."

There was an ice bucket on the counter right by the refrigerator. The corkscrew was inside.

"Half a glass for me," she called. "Unless you want to be my designated driver."

I poured half a glass for her, a slightly fuller one for myself. Then another dollop in mine—I wasn't going anywhere.

"Thanks," she said. When she reached for the glass, the clingy fabric of her white top stretched across her ample chest. I flinched, expecting an errant button to come flying at my face, an accidental discharge.

"No, thank you," I said. "I mean for the goodies. It's very thoughtful."

"There's no good time for it, but it's a terrible time to be alone."

"I don't mind it so much," I said. "Being alone. I have a dog."

"What's his name?"

"Archie. It's not mine. I mean I didn't name him. I adopted him."

"Why do you keep standing there?"

"No reason." I sat back down on the ottoman.

"I used to have a cat," she said. "Puffin. Puffin the Cat, I called her."

"Husband got it?"

"It died."

I sipped my wine. I didn't care much for wine. I took another sip. She scooted forward and peeled the plastic wrapping from the basket. Crackers, a wedge of Brie, some grapes, a couple Granny Smith apples. I went back to the kitchen and fetched a knife for the apples and Brie.

"This'll be my dinner," she said. "I'm on a diet. But the wine, I can't give it up. White wine is very fattening, you know. I never drank when I was married, but now I drink all the time. Well, socially. It's not like I go home and chug a bottle by my lonesome every night."

"Me, too," I said, and took another sip. I nibbled on a cracker. Melody noticed a smear of the soft cheese clinging to her forefinger and the finger disappeared to the second knuckle between those ruby lips. I got up again and trooped into the kitchen, where I'd left the bottle. I brought it back and she held up her glass. "Little more," she said. "More. More. Oh, no, too much, but that's okay. Why don't you sit down? You sit for five seconds, jump up, come back, stand there, like you might have to make a break for it. It's okay; I have no designs. I don't believe in taking advantage of vulnerable people."

"I'm vulnerable?"

"It's all over you, Theodore Ruzak. It exudes from your pores."

I sat on the ottoman and willed myself to be still, particularly my right leg, which tended to pop up and down: a man in complete possession of his faculties.

"So relax, Mr. Ragman. There's no agenda here," she said, and then launched into her agenda: "If you were even halfway serious about it, I've got some free time tomorrow."

"Free time for what?"

"To show you around. Best buyer's market in twenty years.

Foreclosures, fire sales. People are desperate, *desperate,* to sell. What time is it?"

I looked at my watch. "Nine-fifty-three."

"I mean the funeral tomorrow."

"Right."

Her eyes sparkled over the rim of her wineglass.

"You've forgotten the question, haven't you?"

"All my money's tied up in the market," I said. "My broker says to hang in there; you gotta be in for the long haul."

"What was your aunt's name again?"

"Rachel." Ah, God.

"I thought you said it was Regina."

"It is. She went by her middle name."

"Rachel Regina Ruzak? That's so . . ."

"Alliterative."

"Unusual. Been here for twenty years, you'd think I'd know that name. I know practically everybody in town."

"She was kind of a recluse," I said. "Agoraphobic."

"I'm afraid of the dark. Ever since I was a little girl."

"It unnerved me a little tonight, when night fell. Where I live, it's a little brighter, a lot noisier."

"Where's the service? I could meet you there afterward."

"You know, it's hard, like you said. A hard time. I don't think I'd be up to looking at investment properties."

I refilled my glass. She held out hers. We were nearing the bottom of the bottle. It was our only bottle; I didn't figure she'd hang around long without wine nearby. Time to strike while the iron was hot, make some hay while the sun shone.

"I brought along a couple of books," I said. "I haven't had a good nap in five or six years. I like the idea of just lying around and doing nothing. And this is a good place to do that, terrific if the sun decides to come out. You know the owners well? They come down often?"

She shook her head. "It must be a couple years since Tom and Kat came down."

"That long? So who owns that car outside?"

"Tom said it was theirs."

"Tom said?"

"This afternoon, when I called to double-check they weren't in town."

"If they haven't come down in a couple years, how did the car get here?"

"He said she must have driven it down."

"Oh. So if she drove it down, where is she?"

"He doesn't know. They've split. Kat's kind of erratic. He thinks she parked it here and took off to parts unknown."

Unless she's in the trunk, trussed with a Hefty twist tie.

"How do you take off without your car?"

"Maybe she left it here and took a cab to the airport."

"Why leave it here, though?"

"Because you can't take your car on the plane?"

"No, I mean, why not just abandon the car at the airport?"

"Maybe she didn't want anyone to know she went to the airport," she said.

"Why would she want that?"

"How the hell should I know? Are you a consultant or a cop?"

"I'm just curious."

"You've never been married."

"Oh. She's scared. What is he, a wife-beater?"

"I always thought he was pretty nice. Very charming. Smart. Handsome. *Tons* of money. *Tons* of it. Money so old, it has moss growing on it. He's a professor or something in Knoxville." A look came over her face: the lightbulb coming on. "*You're* from Knox-ville."

"Small world, huh?"

"You *are* a cop, aren't you?"

"No." I sighed. "Okay. Sorry. I'm a PI. Katrina Bates was my client. She's disappeared. I'm trying to find her."

She stared at me for a couple of seconds. Then she said, "Is your name really Theodore Ruzak?"

"Yes."

"And the dead aunt?"

"There is no dead aunt."

"And you're not an investment broker?"

"I never technically said I was."

"Why did you lie to me?"

"I didn't know how close your connection was to Tom."

"My connection to Tom matters?"

"It might."

"You think he did something to her."

"I have a working theory."

"Well, I don't know him. Well, I do, in a casual way. They've had me over here for drinks. Took me out once on his boat."

Bing. "Tom has a boat? Where?"

"Here. At the marina."

She downed the dregs of her wine and eyed the empty glass wistfully.

"Come to think of it, he did kind of hit on me once. On the boat. Sort of playful pass, you know, nothing scary or very seri-ous. He likes to flirt, knows women find him attractive. But I was married at the time. I believe in the sanctity of marriage, don't you?"

I nodded. "And life. That, too."

"I've never met a real PI before," she said, and I thought, *And you still haven't.* "Do you carry a gun?"

"I left it in Knoxville."

"You don't look like a PI. You look like . . . oh, I don't know, you're so tall and big, and those sad, soft, puppy-dog eyes."

"PIs have reputations of being a little seedy and cynical and smarmy and hard-edged," I admitted. I thought of Dresden Falks. "Some of it deserved."

"Have you ever killed anyone?"

"Not directly."

She squeezed her thighs together and tugged on the hem of her skirt. Then she hugged her knees, which forced her breasts forward, the cleft between them deepening as she leaned forward, her lips slightly parted.

"Let me have a sip of that," she said, echoing Felicia.

"Of what?" I asked stupidly. The bottle was empty.

"Your wine, dummy."

I held out my glass. As the only flesh-and-blood PI she probably would ever meet, I felt the obligation to set an example, to be an exemplar of PI-hood. *In me, dear lady, chivalry lives on.* Her fingertips brushed mine as she took it, lingered there for a millisecond too long. Our eyes met.

"Are you going to kiss me now, Ragman?" she whispered.

"Yes," I said.

SCENE NINE
The Beach

An Hour Later

I removed my shoes and socks and walked right to the edge, to the end of it, where the rolling water kissed the continent and caressed my bare feet. Far to sea, a storm raged, too far away to hear the thunder, the lightning illuminating the horizon in brief, startling flashes. Onshore, the rain had departed. So had Melody Moy.

Her lips had tasted slightly salty from the crackers, slightly syrupy from the wine, their texture reminding me of crayons, all that lipstick, and her tongue seemed large in my mouth as she dug her fingernails into my scalp, and I placed both hands on her breasts almost immediately and pressed hard, pulling at the buttons, sliding a finger into the little hole between them, pushing my left leg between her bare ones (no one wore panty hose anymore), forcing them apart, and her hands fell to my shoulders and she began to push, breaking the kiss and gasping, "What is this? What is this?" I didn't say anything but was thinking, for some reason, *Fire, fire, fire!* I leaned against her and forced her backward, putting my mouth on hers again with my eyes tightly shut, the ache in my chest clamped just as tightly down. My first kiss was stolen behind some bleachers in junior high school, a girl named Carly, who parted her hair down the middle and who spoke with a slight lisp—"Teddy Ruthak," she called me—and this was taken after several weeks of practicing on my own wrist, and the basic technique probably hadn't changed much in the intervening years. I tried to remember Carly's face, but all that came was her shoulder-length hair, straight, parted in the middle. I tried to remember if her nose crinkled when she smiled. *Give me a sip of that. And this is what I want, damn it. Stop pushing. You've done your agenda. This is mine.* And Melody Moy grabbed my wrists and pulled downward, but I was too strong.

She let go and hit me as hard as she could on the right cheek. I fell away, pulling my hands into my lap, eyes still closed, saying, "I'm sorry, okay? Sorry. It's not you. I didn't mean you. Not you. Not you. Not you." I didn't move, didn't even open my eyes, as she grabbed her purse and the basket—why did she take the basket?— and slammed out the door, and only then did I open my eyes and stare for a few minutes at the imprint of her lips on the empty glass sitting on the coffee table.

SCENE TEN
The Beach

Moments Later

I stripped off my clothes and strode naked into the sea.

SCENE ELEVEN
Lecture Hall

Three Days Later

After the cacophony of slamming books and buzzing, chirping, beeping, rap music–ringing cell phones faded and the last backpack-burdened undergrad had rushed from the room, but before Tom Bates could slide out the side door, I came in and walked down the steps to the front row, where I planted myself in a chair and looked at the dry-erase board and the hundreds of numbers and symbols that filled it, stretching ten feet from edge to edge, a single ineffable equation that, for all I knew, proved something of staggering proportions, on a par with the elegant $E=mc^2$, the only famous mathematical formula I knew beyond □ and that might not qualify as a formula, but only as a symbol.

Tom Bates stepped off the stage and stood beside me, and we stared at the board, like a couple of art aficionados at the Louvre.

"Beautiful, isn't it?" he asked.

"As a sunset," I said. "What's it mean?"

"Your question is a bit nonsensical, Mr. Ruzak. It has no meaning beyond the intrinsic."

"Well," I said. "It wouldn't be the first time."

RICHARD YANCEY

"Poetry of the mind. No. More perfect than poetry, for it is *of* us and yet so totally, beautifully, *outside* us."

"You like poetry, too?" I asked. I thought of the earthy odes tucked away in his sock drawer.

"I write it. I've been published in the *Poetry Review.*"

"I never got beyond the 'Roses are red' stage."

He nodded. I tensed, waiting for him to lay a line of his Pulitzer Prize–winning poetry on me.

He didn't. He sat beside me and said, "You've found my wife."

"No. But I found a piece of her."

I pulled the paper sack from my briefcase and set it on the desktop in front of him. He didn't open it.

"Can't be a large piece," he said. "A finger or a toe?"

"Her sunglasses. Chanel. She was wearing them the last time I saw her."

"Hmm. You found them at the beach house?"

"On the boat. In this little space beside the compartment with the life jackets."

"I believe she had more than one pair, Mr. Ruzak."

"'Had' is past tense."

He nodded. "*Has* more than one pair."

"Identical ones? I remember these glasses."

"She probably lost them and got a replacement."

"She would have to."

"'Have to'?"

"They're prescription."

"Car abandoned at vacation house, plus prescription glasses, plus boat equals murder?"

"You're the math whiz; you tell me."

"I didn't murder my wife, Mr. Ruzak."

144

"I have a theory," I said. I nodded toward the board. "You like theories, right?"

"Theorems," he said. He fingered the edge of the fold on the bag.

"Don't touch," I said. "They'll want to dust them."

"You've gone to the police, then?"

"We could both go," I suggested.

"You were going to share a theory."

"These things happen," I said. "Everybody gets emotional, rationality gets tossed out on its ear, and we rarely recognize our own hypocrisy. If you thought she was having an affair and also thought she was stripping you of everything you had just because genius demands its own latitudes, in the heat of the moment, things could quickly spin out of control. Happens to everybody. Even geniuses have a hypothalamus."

"Animating spirit," he said softly.

"What's that?"

"The literal meaning of *genius*: 'animating spirit.'"

"Oh. You bet. So sometimes the spirit gets a little more animated than normal, a little too animated for its own good."

"You think I killed Katrina. You honestly think I killed my wife."

"You're not interested in what I think, Mr. Bates."

"Mr. Ruzak, I'm astounded by it."

"Be interested in what I know. And here's what I know: A few days after her marriage totally collapses, Katrina vanishes into thin air, on the very day she's arranged for you to swing by and pick up your stuff. She called me from your house at twelve-thirty-six that day; you arrived there at twelve-forty-five, eight minutes later—"

"Nine minutes, Mr. Ruzak," he said, correcting me.

"Nine minutes," I said. *Thanks,* pi *man.* "She wasn't there, you said, and she didn't show for our meeting."

"Why was she meeting you?"

"I'm not sure. She didn't say."

"You told me she wasn't your client anymore."

"She wasn't."

"So this was a social get-together."

"I'm not sure what she had in mind."

"Mr. Ruzak, were you and my wife seeing each other?"

"Of course not."

"You were fucking my wife, weren't you?"

"I would never do that with a client," I said. What was going on? How, in a matter of seconds, had I morphed from interrogator into suspect?

"She wasn't your client," he said.

"I was trying to give you the facts, Mr. Bates."

"That *is* a fact. She wasn't your client. Beyond the fact of her 'disappearance,' it's the most troubling fact of the whole affair. She fired you, then makes dates to see you. She flees town, and you pursue her to Tybee and trespass upon my private property, looking for evidence that I did something to her. These facts don't indicate a man who 'hardly knew' someone."

I cleared my throat. "I didn't trespass. I paid two thousand dollars for one night. And I was not personally involved with your wife. I don't know how to prove a negative."

"Yet you've come here today demanding that I do. I can't prove I had nothing to do with Kat's disappearance."

"But you could help prove that was her decision. Have you called the bank? The cell-phone company? She wouldn't get very far without money, and the odds are she wouldn't travel without means of communication. You could do that."

"Why do you assume I haven't?"

"So you have?"

"Whether I have or not is none of your business. Why are you doing this, Mr. Ruzak? This is a private matter between my wife and me, and who are you to bull your way into our lives like this? What is the meaning of it?"

"That's a good question, Mr. Bates. Maybe it has no meaning beyond the intrinsic."

A dark look passed over his face. Like a kid throwing a grown-up's favorite maxim right back in his face, I had crossed a line. I had stepped on the toes of an ego the size of King Kong.

"Alive or dead, I'm going to find her," I said softly.

"Your bravado is touching, Mr. Ruzak, but I sincerely doubt that you will."

"Because her body is at the bottom of the Atlantic?"

"Because she's smarter than you. In many ways, she smarter than both of us. You and I are incapable of proving a negative, but Katrina's been doing it for over twenty years."

"You're talking about your marriage?"

"I'm talking about her marriage."

SCENE TWELVE
Chesapeake's Restaurant

The Next Day

Detective Meredith Black of the Knoxville PD ordered the grilled swordfish with fresh steamed vegetables. I ordered fried shrimp and hush puppies, with fried okra on the side.

"In the still of the night," she said smiling, "can you hear them hardening?" Her smile was broad, bright, and brisk, teeth disappearing as quickly as they appeared, like with Dustin Hoffman's drag queen in that movie *Tootsie*. Though Meredith was a lot better-looking than Dustin. Dark hair, darker eyes, high cheekbones—I suspected Cherokee in her lineage.

"What?" I asked.

"Your arteries."

"The cutoff is forty."

"Forty what?"

"Years. On my fortieth birthday, I'm going strictly white meat, low starch, low cal, and I'm giving up all things fried."

"Think you can?"

"Think I'll try."

"Every once in awhile, I break down and gorge on those hot brownie sundaes from Buddy's."

I sipped my sweet iced tea to distract my mind from the image of Meredith Black gorging.

"So what do you think?" I asked.

"It is a little odd," she said.

"But not enough for a search warrant."

"There's no probable cause. No one's even reported her missing."

"What about me?"

"You haven't filed a report."

"I could. I will."

"And then we send someone over there, Tom gives us the same spiel he gave you, and we still don't have probable cause."

"What about the abandoned car?" I asked. "The empty house. The glasses on the boat?"

"She dumped the car at the house, took a cab to the airport, boarded a plane to parts unknown."

"And the glasses?"

"Lost on the boat, just like Tom said."

"Where they lay for two years, out in the elements, until I found them looking good as new."

"Suspicion isn't evidence, Teddy."

Our food came. Meredith chewed vigorously, as if she had some underlying issues with swordfish.

"There's a tipping point," I said. "When the last itty-bitty fact pushes things from odd coincidence to damning circumstance."

"Hey, I like that," she said. "Except the 'itty-bitty' part. I haven't heard that phrase since my grandmother died."

"Katrina kicks Tom out of the house. Vows to destroy him and all he holds dear. A few days later, she goes missing without a trace and her car turns up abandoned several hundred miles away."

"That would be a trace. The car."

"Plus the fact that around the same time, Tom received information that she might be having an affair herself. Or he interpreted it that way. Plus the fact that he paid a lot of money for that information or maybe for information we don't have yet, something he would be desperate to hide. Plus the fact that once he knew I was snooping around, he dispatched a lackey to offer me a way out of my professional difficulties with the state."

She was slowly shaking her head.

"Maybe I'm not as good at math as you."

"And neither of us is better at it than Tom Bates. Can I ask you a professional question?"

"No, but you can ask a question about my profession."

Bing: Out came the teeth. *Bing:* gone again.

"What more would you guys need to open a case on this?"

"Turn up a witness." She pulled the last hunk of fish meat from the skewer with her fingers and popped the whole thing into her mouth. Then she licked her fingertips. "Or a body. A body would be good. A dead one or a living one, doesn't matter. Bring me a body, Ruzak."

SCENE THIRTEEN
The Office

That Afternoon

Felicia had left a message in the middle of my blotter, scrawled on my yellow legal pad, which made me wonder why she'd been sitting at my desk while I was out. What was wrong with her desk? After screwing my courage to the sticking place, I dialed the number.

"It's me," I said. "Ruzak."

"If that's your real name," said Melody Moy. "Why'd you do this, Teddy?"

"To say I'm sorry."

"Nobody's sent me roses since '05."

"I am, though," I said. "Sorry. I guess I could blame it on the wine. I'm not a very accomplished drinker."

"You're not very accomplished at a lot of things."

"I'm highly sensitive to karmic disturbances. There's an answering vibration, like a psychic tuning fork."

"What does that mean?"

"This case, or noncase, or whatever the hell it is, created this kind of rupture, and unfortunately I tumbled into the chasm."

"This isn't getting better," she said. "You should have stuck with 'I'm sorry.'"

"I'm sorry."

"I'll be honest with you: I left understanding completely why you've never been married."

"Maybe I'm the kind of person who can learn only by doing."

"And you've suffered for lack of a practice dummy?"

"Oh, I would never do something like that. That's pretty weird. Sad, too."

Felicia appeared in the doorway and leaned against the jamb, arms over chest, ankles crossed. She was wearing a bright green skirt and matching pumps. Jadish earrings and necklace with fat blocks of green rock dangling from her lobes and graceful neck.

"Have you found the missing lady?" asked Melody Moy.

"Not yet."

"Do you want me to make some discrete inquiries? My cousin's wife works for TSA. . . . Maybe she could pull some manifests."

I didn't think that would amount to a hill of beans, but she didn't know what I knew.

"Hey, you don't have to," I said.

"Not what I asked, Ragman."

"Sure. That would be terrific. Every little bit helps."

I said good-bye and hung up the phone. Felicia hung by the door. She didn't say anything.

"That was Melody Moy," I said.

"I know."

"The real estate lady."

"She has a name like a cartoon character. One of Batman's girlfriends or a gangster's moll."

"There's a pattern I've noticed," I said. "Girls I've kissed. All their names end in a *y*. Tiffany, Melody, even Carly."

"Who is Carly?"

"An eighth grader."

"Jesus Christ, Ruzak."

"No, I mean I kissed her in the eighth grade."

"What about Amanda? That's an *a*."

"I'm not counting her."

"How come?"

"It was more like she kissed me. Okay. So the pattern is names that end in a vowel."

"And that girl from your first case—what was her name?"

"Susan." How did she know I'd kissed Susan? "Okay. Names with at least two syllables."

"You know what you do? Cherry-pick facts to fit your premises."

"Everybody does that."

"What did Detective Black say?"

"Not much they can do without evidence."

"Huh. Never holds *you* back."

"Is there a reason for this?" I asked. "Really."

"Why so tense today, Ruzak?"

"No reason. I'm losing my dog, my business, and possibly my mind. Other than that, I'm good."

She stepped into the room, and for the first time I saw the slip of paper in her hand. She dropped it on top of the yellow pad.

"What's this?" I asked.

"The number for Katrina Bates's father."

"She hates him though."

"According to . . ."

"The suspect."

She tapped the end of her nose.

"You may be distantly related," I said.

"Who?"

"You and Melody Moy. Both your noses crinkle when you smile or laugh. That's got to be genetic."

"I don't like the idea of you hitting on my cousin, Ruzak."

"She didn't like it much, either."

The outer door swung open and Walter Hinton stepped into the room, a uniformed cop in tow. He walked straight to my desk without so much as a nod in Felicia's direction and planted himself in my visitor's chair, balancing his briefcase on his thighs. Felicia didn't move. I didn't move. The cop by the door didn't move. And now, planted, Hinton didn't move.

"Mr. Ruzak, I have a subpoena."

"Surprise, surprise," Felicia murmured in a pretty good imitation of Gomer Pyle. Hinton ignored her. He was staring at me. Felicia was staring at him. I was staring at Hinton, and the cop was staring at nothing.

"Every file. Every scrap of paper. Every hard drive and computer disc and CD and portable media."

"Okay," I said. "Anything else?"

"Yes. The contents of your desk. And your secretary's desk."

"Down to the staples? What do the staples prove?"

"We've gone out of business," Felicia said.

"We have?" I asked.

"There are no files," she said pleasantly. "No files, no discs, no flash drives. You're welcome to the hard drive, but the only things on there are my mother's peanut butter pie recipe and some pictures of Ruzak's dog."

"Where are the files?" he growled.

"Destroyed," she answered. "You caught us in the middle of mopping up."

"I'm taking the computer and the check register. You haven't destroyed that, have you?"

"I would have if I could have. Ruzak took it home to balance it and the dog ate it."

"The dog ate his homework?"

"He's an adoptee," I explained. "There're lingering behavioral issues."

In the outer room, the cop stifled a laugh.

"I'll go to the bank," Hinton vowed.

"For what?" asked Felicia. "What will that establish?"

"You're taking people's money illegally!"

"Oh, Jesus, Hinton," she said. "It's not like Ruzak was transplanting hearts without a medical license or something. Let's keep it in perspective."

"None of this matters," Hinton said.

"Then why are you here?" Felicia asked.

"I'll have you locked down so tight, you won't be able to swing a dead cat in this town without my knowing about it," he said to me.

"That's ugly," she said.

Hinton stood up. I stood up. Felicia and the cop didn't stand up because they were already standing up.

"You may stay during the confiscation," he said. "Up to you. We don't want any trouble, but we are authorized to use force if necessary."

Felicia took a step toward him. I raised my hand. She stopped. Now everybody was looking at me: Felicia, Hinton, the cop.

"That won't be necessary," I said. "You're just trying to do the right thing, Walter, same as I am."

"I'm not the same as you," he snarled.

"Same, only different."

"I think you may just be the stupidest man I've ever met, Mr. Ruzak."

I eased the piece of paper with the phone number on it from the desktop to my pocket. Hinton was too upset to notice. I didn't doubt if there weren't witnesses present, he would have taken his briefcase upside my head. It may sound weird, but at that moment I actually felt sorry for Walter Hinton. Evil may thwart our empathy, but madness doth our pity loose.

SCENE FOURTEEN
Penthouse Suite

Two Days Later

An attractive woman who was probably born within five years of me opened the door wearing tennis gear and holding a bottle of Fiji water. Her eyes were an interesting gray, her hair a boring blond, cut shoulder-length and pulled into a ponytail that bounced when she walked. She was tall, close to six feet, I guessed, trim, long-legged, and she smelled of sunscreen. Her vibe was more West Coast than East, but this was New York City, the white-hot center of the melting pot.

She led me into a study tastefully decorated with an old-world flavor, not too mod but also not too staid. The furniture was light on the knickknacks, the walls easy on the artwork, and the chairs were comfortable. There were no pictures of family.

She said her name was Anna. I said my name was Teddy.

"Would you like a drink, Teddy?" she asked.

"Love one," I said. "One of those Fijis would be great, if you got another."

She said she did, and left to get it. I stood by the window and admired the view. She came back and handed me the water, and I admired her smile.

"How was your flight?" she asked. She sounded genuinely interested, not like she was making conversation.

"Hit some turbulence near the end," I said. "I made the mistake of ordering coffee and it ended up all over the guy in front of me."

"Oh no!" She laughed politely.

"He was very understanding."

"And you learned a lesson."

"The hard way."

"Often the best way."

"Often the Ruzak way."

"What is that name? Russian?"

"Polish."

"A Polish PI."

"Sounds like the beginning of a joke," I said.

"I think that's so horrible. Ethnic jokes."

"Things have tightened up on them, but sometimes the best humor is rooted in pain."

"Is that a quote or something?"

"Something."

An older man came into the room, maybe a couple inches taller than Anna. I was guessing seventy, based on his daughter's age, but a fantastic seventy, a lion-in-winter kind of guy, with just the hint of a paunch and a full head of salt-and-pepper hair, gelled and fashionably long, combed back from his finely formed forehead. His eyes were a glittering emerald green, his voice soft, his handshake hard.

"Alistair Lynch," he said.

"Theodore Ruzak," I said.

"Ruzak. That Ukrainian?"

"Polish."

"Polish! And you're from Knoxville."

"Born here, though."

"New York?"

"Queens."

"Not Chicago? Lot of Poles in Chicago."

"I might have a cousin or two that way."

"What do you think of the Cubs' chances this year?"

"Pitching's the issue."

"Pitching is always the issue. You've met Anna."

"She brought me this water."

"How did you get from Queens to Knoxville?"

"In my dad's car and a U-Haul trailer. He was a salesman and moved around a lot."

"What did he sell?"

"Name it."

"You didn't follow in his footsteps."

"Neither one of us wanted me to."

"You take after your mother's side."

"Afraid so."

"Why afraid?"

"Most of that side died of cancer at an early age."

"It's all about risk factors. Do you smoke?"

"Once, in the seventh grade. Peer pressure."

"Weight's the biggest. You should lose about twenty pounds."

"Working on that."

"Really?"

"No. Not really. I've got a six-year plan."

"What's your plan?"

"Cold turkey on the fried foods in six years."

"Anna, could you get me a drink? Have a seat, Ruzak. How was your flight?"

"Just a minor spill over Virginia."

"That reminds me of a joke."

I waited for him to tell it. Nothing. Was he waiting for me to say "Love to hear it"? Finally, I gave up and got down to brass tacks.

"Thanks for agreeing to see me," I said.

"Katrina is my only child."

As if on cue, the woman who was young enough to be his child came back with his drink.

"I'm off," she told him. "Dinner with the Trumps tonight at seven. Don't forget." She kissed him on the cheek. Said she was delighted to have met me. I thanked her for the water.

She left. I watched her leave. He watched me watch her leave.

"Trumps, as in *the* Trumps?" I asked.

"More her connection than mine. I'm becoming less and less sociable as I get older."

"That's pretty common."

"Do you think so?"

"Maybe it's a function of diminishing energy."

"In my case, it may be a function of my being an irascible ass."

"Well," I said. "Everybody's different."

"Some more than others."

"Most more than others."

He laughed, for some reason. "You're not my idea of a private eye at all."

"That's sort of an auxiliary mission of mine: blasting stereotypes."

"The primary one being catching the bad guy."

"Right. Or I wouldn't be a private eye."

"And you honestly think Tom did something to her."

"I do."

He nodded, sipped his drink, eyes green as a cat's on me.

"What do the authorities think?" he asked.

"They're reading the same book, but they're a chapter or two behind."

"He's a very clever man."

"And he knows it."

"You're hoping that will undo him."

"Goes before a fall."

"To the ancient Greeks, you know, it was the greatest sin."

"Worse than murder?"

"When you think about it, it's a kind of suicide."

I thought I could think about it for a hundred years and wouldn't arrive within a thousand miles of that conclusion, but I didn't say anything.

"I never liked him," Alistair Lynch said. "A brutally selfish man, not at all like his father. His father and I were friends. Not close friends, but we belonged to some of the same organizations. Brilliant—I mean Tom—but pushy, and operatically arrogant. And of course his struggles with monogamy—unforgivable," he said with a straight face.

"But they stayed married for twenty years."

"The first ten owing entirely to my daughter's inestimable will. The last ten to inertia. And, I'll confess, to certain deficiencies in Katrina's psychology."

"Picking open old scabs."

"Not a pleasant analogy, but yes, I was not faithful to the girl's mother."

"Tom said she caught you in bed with the nanny."

"She wasn't the nanny. She was Katrina's violin teacher. Katrina was twelve. Afterward, we traded the tutor for a therapist."

"For you or for her?"

"Ah, Mr. Ruzak, really. It was a very long time ago."

"Ever see him lose his temper?"

"Once. He threw a chair through a window."

"Why?"

"I can't recall all the details—it's been fifteen years at least—but I believe it had something to do with a colleague receiving some honor that Tom thought was his just due. The fit didn't last long. No more than five minutes, and he was quite calm and collected afterward. Apologized. I do recall Katrina being a bit shaken by it."

"Because it came out of the blue?"

"He never struck me as a violent man."

"And he never struck her?"

"Not that I'm aware of. I doubt she would have told me if he had."

"Is it plausible to you, him hurting her, say, after being pushed to the wall by something?"

"I can imagine it, if his ego was sufficiently threatened, as in the incident with the chair."

"More than a threat to divorce him and take all his money?"

"Oh, that was a threat laid down early and often, repeated so much, he hardly took it seriously."

"What if he found out *she* was having an affair?"

He nodded. "That might do it."

"He explodes and throws the metaphorical chair through the window."

If it bothered him that I had just compared his only daughter to a piece of furniture, he didn't show it.

"He said the two of you haven't spoken in years," I said.

"Yes. So I was surprised when you called. Why did you think the girl would contact me?"

"It was more a hope than a thought."

"That he was lying about our estrangement?"

"That she was alive."

"She cut off all contact when I married Anna."

"The final straw?"

"Anna is six years younger than Katrina."

"And the tutor was six years older."

A nod. "The circle comes round."

I didn't get it. I kept saying things, not completely on purpose, that would offend most people, but this Alistair Lynch reacted as if we were still discussing the Cubbies. On the one hand, I admired his self-possession. On the other, I felt the need to take a long, hot shower, as if I had come in contact with something fetid.

"We could have covered all this on the phone yesterday," I said. "Why did you ask me to fly up here, Mr. Lynch?"

"I wanted to show you this."

He went to the mantel and picked up a manila envelope. Handed it to me.

"Last fall, after eight years of total silence, this."

Inside the envelope were two things: a note written on Katrina's stationery (KLB was printed on the top in fancy script) and a small square-headed key. The note read "Alistair, keep this for me. K."

"She never called me 'Dad,'" he said.

"What's the key to?"

"I don't know."

"And you never asked her about it? After eight years of nothing, she sends you a key and a cryptic note, and you don't ask?"

"I suppose I assumed one day she would ask for it."

"You suppose you assumed?"

"I find drama distasteful, Mr. Ruzak. And Katrina was not

merely dramatic; she was melodramatic. I was surprised when she chose law school over a career in acting. She had the gift, you know. She played the role of Regina in her high school production of *The Little Foxes,* and she was, in my biased opinion, brilliant."

I dropped the key and the note back into the envelope.

"Can I keep this?" I asked.

"It's why I invited you up here."

My bottle was empty. His glass was dry. He rose. I rose. He walked me to the door.

"Speaking of the theater, are you familiar with *Hamlet,* Mr. Ruzak?" he asked. "She may have been hoist with her own petard."

"How so?"

"Her penchant for the grand gesture, the attention-seeking melodramatics. If he has done something to her, she has come to his aid. She's laid the groundwork for him. It wouldn't be the first time she's taken off into the blue like a child running away from home so Daddy will come looking."

At the door, he turned to me, and I looked for some kind of emotion in his eyes—concern, anger, guilt, sorrow, something, anything. There was nothing.

"It was children more than the affairs," he said.

"What was?"

"Or the lack thereof. Tom wanted them, particularly a son, and she refused. Absolutely refused."

"Why?"

"She never gave her reasons, at least not to me."

"The best way to punish him for cheating?"

"Or to protect them."

"Who?"

"The unborn children. Perhaps she was afraid she would have a daughter."

"And one day their daughter walks in on Tom with the nanny."

"Violin tutor."

"Either one."

"Yes." He seemed pleased I understood. "You're quite perceptive, Mr. Ruzak. For a Pole."

"Like I said," I replied. "Blasting stereotypes."

SCENE FIFTEEN
La Guardia Airport

Three Hours Later

We were fifteen minutes from boarding when my cell phone rang.

"Well?" Felicia asked.

"He's pals with Donald Trump."

"Wow. That should crack the case."

"He also doesn't seem concerned in the least."

"For him, she's been missing a very long time, Ruzak."

"He said Tom has an explosive temper. And he gave me a key."

"A key to what?"

"I don't know."

"He didn't say?"

"He doesn't know, either. Katrina sent it to him a few months back."

"The plot thickens. She called this afternoon."

"Katrina?"

"No, dummy, that detective woman." Felicia rarely referred to Meredith Black by name. "They've had a sit-down with Tom. He doesn't know nothing from nothing. Thinks she's run off and she'll be back. Doesn't know how, why, or when the car got to Tybee and is clueless about the sunglasses you found on the boat. They asked to take a look around his house; he refused. Said they can search when they come back with a warrant."

"Did they?"

"She said the judge won't go for it, not without probable cause. He's done it before, you know."

"Done what? Killed somebody?"

"No, Ruzak. Reported her missing. A couple of times."

"But not this time."

"He told the detective woman this time he's more relieved than worried. Those other times, he actually had hopes the marriage would work. So they're stuck."

"Maybe this key is the key."

"A little insurance policy? But why send it to the old man? She can't stand him."

"Something Tom knows. He'd never suspect she'd give it to Alistair for safekeeping."

"She also said they've checked with the airports and every rental-car place within a two-hundred-mile radius of Savannah."

"Let me guess," I said.

"Nada," she said, not letting me guess. "No record of a Katrina Bates renting a car or boarding a flight."

"Bank records," I said. "Cell-phone records."

"Can't without a warrant."

"If you were innocent," I said, "wouldn't you tell the cops, 'Sure, you bet, have a look around the place'? "Here're her bank statements; here're her cell bills. Here's a list of names of everyone she's met in the past three years. Here's a list of her favorite vacation spots.'"

"Most people would," she said. "Tom Bates is not most people.

She barely had time to flash her badge before he lawyered up. Oh, that reminds me, the reason she called. She needs you to go down and give a statement."

"A statement of what?"

"History, Ruzak. How this played out from the day Katrina Bates hired you. What you know. An official statement."

The desk clerk announced we would be boarding shortly. I stood up and walked to the windows to eyeball the plane. For some reason, it helped my preflight jitters when my untrained eye detected no apparent defects in the plane, like a four-inch crack in the wing, and saw no mechanics fiddling around in the undercarriage.

"How's Archie?" I asked her.

"Chewing contentedly on a bone."

"Okay if I pick him up tomorrow?"

"I'll just take him with me in the morning."

"Should we go to the office? Hinton might be watching."

"Why would Hinton be watching?"

"He's doggedly persistent."

"Like a certain researcher and analyst I know."

My focus shifted from the plane beyond the pane to my own wispy reflection in it. Ghostlike, insubstantial. A faded memory of myself.

"I'm not going to find her," I said to it.

She thought I was talking to her. "You honestly thought you would?"

"Not all the research is finished, but the analysis pretty much is. She's dead, Felicia. She's dead, and by now her bones have been picked clean by the scavengers that patrol the continental shelf."

"Don't go all soft on me now, Ruzak."

"It's over. Done."

"Right. Tomorrow you hand over the key to the detective, give your statement, and work on your résumé."

"It's just there was . . . until right now . . . this sliver, this knot at the end of the rope I was hanging on to. That maybe this bad feeling was just a feeling and she was sipping cocktails on the beach in Rio."

"Still an outside chance of that. Maybe you ought to book a flight to Rio."

As if cued, the clerk made the general boarding call.

"You have to go," she said. "See you in the morning."

"Here's the problem," I said. "I want to find the truth, but I want the truth I find to be the truth I want to find. It *is* about me, this Galahad thing. She isn't the only one with a savior complex. You know, we think of the truth as a light-giving source, but sometimes it just plunges the whole room into darkness. The answer we find isn't the answer we're hoping for, like the prayer that goes unanswered. The answer is in the box."

"What box?"

"Whatever box this little key opens. Maybe it's her itinerary. Maybe she left behind a manifesto, and explanation of why she took off."

"Get on the plane, Ruzak."

"He's lying. I should go back and lean on him. What kind of father doesn't hear from his kid in eight years, gets a key in the mail with a cryptic note, and doesn't pick up the phone and ask 'So what is the deal with this friggin' key and cryptic note?' He's in on it."

"He's conspired with his son-in-law in the murder of his only child?"

"Maybe not the murder. Maybe the cover-up."

"Oh, come on, Teddy. Cut it out and get on the plane."

"Or it could be a setup. Manufactured evidence. Tom put something in the box and sent Alistair the key, pretending it was from Katrina. But why would he do that? Why not just create a fake good-bye letter and send it to him?"

"Or simply mail one to himself. Or forge a note and leave it on the fridge. Or send one to *you,* her new best friend. I'm hanging up. Board the plane, Ruzak. You're coming home."

That's it, I thought as I walked down the ramp. The astonishing thing was hardly astonishing at all when you looked at the facts: Katrina Bates was not going home. No kids, no siblings, a father who had abandoned her and a husband who had betrayed her—even if she wasn't at the bottom of the Atlantic, she wasn't going home, because there was no home for her to go to. I had cast myself as the knight riding to her rescue, but in either scenario it wasn't Katrina Bates who needed rescuing. She was either beyond it or in no need of it. The casting was all wrong: I wasn't the knight; I was the fool.

SCENE SIXTEEN
The Sterchi Building

Four Hours Later

I expected to see him, and there he was.

"He's not here, Whittaker," I said.

"I know." He fell into step with me as I dragged myself toward the elevator. "Where is he?"

"Gone."

"So you actually did it? You gave him to someone else?"

"What's it matter, Whit? Maybe I took him out and shot him in a ditch. The dog is gone, I'm in compliance, and you can move on to the next crisis, like fixing my leaky faucet."

"You have a leaky faucet?"

"No, just making a point."

"Did you take him to the pound? I'd like to know."

"Because?"

"I'm not heartless, Ruzak. I'm not a monster. It's not as if I wanted something bad to happen to that dog."

"You want him, don't you?"

"I was going to say that if you haven't found a suitable home for him. . . ."

"So you *have* been sneaking in my place and playing with him."

"How would you like it, being cooped up all day with no one to play with?"

"Maybe the issue isn't *his* lack of a playmate."

The doors opened. His eyes narrowed.

"I don't like you," he said.

"That's okay," I said. "Neither did the dog."

SCENE SEVENTEEN
On Kingston Pike

The Next Morning

I was sitting in my Sentra when the call came. I didn't need to look at the LCD to know who it was.

I hit the talk button and said, "I'm a fool."

"I'll alert the media," Felicia said. "Where the hell are you?"

"I couldn't sleep last night. I couldn't sleep, so I stayed up with the file and the note and the key, and one thing I couldn't figure is why she wouldn't tell him what the key was to. She's squirreled something away and sends the key to her dad because Tom wouldn't suspect that connection, just in case something happened to her, but she doesn't tell him where to find the thing she's hidden. Why would she do that? On the off chance the cops interview him when she goes missing and he says 'Hey, wait a minute. I did get this weird key, but she didn't tell me what it goes to. It might be useful'? Then I thought maybe he lied to me. Maybe he does know what it goes to but for some reason won't tell me. But if that were true, why give me the thing in the first place? Why invite me up to New York just to give it to me? So I spread it all out on my bed—the file, my notes, the envelope, the note, the key—and about three A.M. it hits me."

"What hit you, Ruzak?" She sounded very tired.

"She didn't hand deliver it to him. She mailed it. So that's where I am."

"The post office?"

"The Mailbox Etc. place on Kingston Pike. It's right there in black and white. Well, she used a blue pen. The return address. Even the box number. It was staring me in the face the whole time. So that's where I am."

"And?"

"It's here. All of it. Pictures of Tom with Kinsey doing . . . well, you can imagine what they're doing. And a diary or kind of daybook, I guess, in Katrina's handwriting, a brief history of her marriage, the affairs, the fights, the threats—the acid-in-her-face remark, things like that. I haven't read the whole thing, just kind of skimmed it, but it ends with her saying if something happens to her, it's gotta be Tom. 'Look to Tom. Look to my husband.'"

"Probable cause," she said.

"I'm heading over right now to turn it over to Meredith."

"And we pray the ol' professor has gotten sloppy."

"When hope of rescue dies, we labor for justice."

"A quote?"

"You bet. Freshly minted."

SCENE EIGHTEEN
The Office

Two Weeks Later

Meredith Black leaned back in the visitor's chair, crossed her legs, and smiled at me. I wasn't sure, but thought I was supposed to give an appreciative, if furtive, glance at her legs. I complied, just in case.

"This conversation never took place," she said.

"What conversation?" I asked.

"Oh, Ruzak. Ever the scamp. Have you heard from the DA's office yet?"

I shook my head.

"You will," she said. "You're a witness, so I shouldn't be telling you all this."

"Then don't."

"No withdrawals from any of the bank accounts. No calls from the cell phone after she called you at the Tomato Head. Blood traces in the kitchen. Blood traces in the trunk of the Mercedes. Blood traces on the boat. Even microscopic amounts on the sunglasses. DNA testing will take awhile, but you and I know whose blood it is. Oh, and we found your case file, hidden inside the bedroom closet. You wanna know what's underlined three times? 'K.B. having illicit liaison with BF.'"

I closed my eyes. The knot on the end of my rope slipped as my conscious mind looked the truth square in the face, a face with which my subconscious was intimately familiar.

"Weapon?" I asked.

"Hard to tell without a body. No residue on any of the kitchen knives—we think he did her in the kitchen—but guess what? The poker is missing."

"The poker?"

"The poker by the fireplace in the living room. It's gone."

"The body? You won't need it?"

She shrugged. "It might wash up onshore one day. It happens. But the DA thinks we have enough. We're picking him up this afternoon."

I took a deep breath.

"Thanks, Meredith."

"No, Mr. Ruzak. Thank you. Without your dogged persistence, the bastard might have gotten away with it."

"'Dogged persistence,'" I echoed. "That's what it's all about, isn't it?"

"Most of it. The rest is luck."

"Which he's run out of."

"More like he ran into something: the brick wall called Teddy Ruzak."

"He'll hire the best lawyers money can buy."

"Already has."

"And they'll say it's a purely circumstantial case. You don't even have a body."

"Well, get off your ass and find us one."

I got off it and walked her to the door. Felicia saw us and pointedly turned her back to open an empty filing cabinet.

"What's going on?" Meredith asked. She pointed at the sign on our door: OUT OF BUSINESS.

"A bureaucratic glitch with the state," I replied. "We're working it out."

"Doggedly?"

"And persistently."

"Good," Meredith Black said. "We need more dicks like you."

I closed the door behind her. Her heels clicked in the echoey stairwell. Behind me, Felicia said, "'More dicks like you.'"

"I'm not a dick," I said.

"That's right," she said. "You're a fool."

ACT THREE

The Crime

SCENE ONE
Offices of the Velman Group, LLC

Three Weeks Later

The Velman Group occupied the entire seventeenth floor of the First Tennessee Bank Building on Gay Street, the tallest building in Knoxville, a glittering edifice of reflective blue glass, designed maybe as an architectural reflection of the river to which the entire state owed so much, a rigid blue tribute not far from the shores of its inspiration, not so rigid and not nearly so blue.

I stepped off the elevators into the reception area a little after 9:00 A.M., wearing a tailored suit that had cost a bundle of my dead mother's money back in the early days of my agency, when my hopes (and my bank balance) were high. Most of that money (and hope) was gone, like my mother. Time to dispose of the one thing I had left: my pride.

A receptionist, a bleached-out, big-haired blonde with large, expressive eyes and an obscenely augmented chest, sat behind a chest-high desk on the opposite wall, beneath the company name in large gold letters. I told her who I was. She asked whom I had come to see. I told her, and she asked me to sign the book, which I did, in very small letters, and I felt like a big man trying to hide behind a sapling. She gestured to the row of chairs pushed against the wall and invited me to have a seat. I flipped through a two-month-old issue of a magazine called *Hot Rodder*. It featured glossy photographs of tricked-out cars and scantily clad girls, most of the cladding being cutoff jeans and plaid halter tops that accentuated their surgically enhanced breasts. They reminded me of the receptionist sitting a dozen feet away. Maybe that was how Dres found her: saw her picture and contacted the magazine. I wondered if it was true that the last receptionist had been fired because she didn't measure up to the Felicia standard. Talk about unintended consequences and the anonymous victims we leave in our wakes!

I waited forty-five minutes, tossed the magazine on the coffee table, and went back to the receptionist and asked how much longer I would be forced to wait, because I was a busy man with pressing concerns and I couldn't wait all day. She picked up the phone and whispered into the receiver, a hand cupped around the mouthpiece. Five more minutes, I was told. Would I like a cup of coffee or a bottle of Evian? I took the Evian.

Fifteen minutes later, Dresden Falks burst through the doors leading into the inner sanctum of the Velman Group, his entire countenance lighted up, absolutely glowing with pleasure. He grabbed my hand and pumped hard, his left cupping my elbow.

"Ruzak, you son of a bitch. Sorry about the wait. Hey, Tammy, babe, hold my calls, will ya?"

I followed him through the doors, down a long hallway, past heavy unmarked doors, the thick carpeting absorbing the sound of our passing, and I was reminded of that creepy hotel in *The Shining*. We turned a couple of corners, traversed a couple more identical hallways with identical heavy unmarked doors, until we reached one that he threw open, revealing a small office with windows facing west toward World's Fair Park and the university. Dresden Falks's desk was as neat as mine was messy, the bookshelves behind it displaying a couple of baseball trophies (he went to college on a scholarship, he proudly told me) and pictures of him with prominent local politicians. He fell into the large leather executive chair that was too big for the desk, shot out his cuffs, and waved me to the visitor's chair, which was too small. I placed my sweating bottle of water on the bare desktop. Sometimes the smallest of paybacks can bring the greatest satisfaction.

"So I'm a little bothered by the receptionist," I said.

"Me, too, but she's married."

"What happened to her?"

"Boob job."

"No, I'm talking about the other one. The reject from the ugly factory."

"Told you." He made a slicing motion across his throat.

"And that really happened because you saw Felicia?"

"What do you think?"

"I'd rather think practically anything but that."

"Relax. I was kidding. You want to know the truth, she had this kind of stalker personality, couldn't peel her offa me. It got creepy; I got rid of her. Upgraded to Tammy out there. Seriously, if you're in the market, the old one's kind of your type. Big, dumb, and naïve as a tenth grader."

"I'm sort of involved right now."

"No kid?" He seemed incredulous. "Not foxy Felicia."

"Lady named Melody, down Savannah way."

"Ah, Ruzak, you oughtta shop closer to home. Those long-distance relationships—they never work."

"It's still in the nascent stages."

"Still in the what stages?"

"I've this habit of reading the dictionary in the john."

"Why am I not surprised?"

"Since childhood. She's the one who pointed me to the boat."

"Boat?"

"Tom's boat. And you're the one who pointed to the town where the boat is."

He held up a manicured hand with a platinum pinkie ring.

"Okay now, Ted, you know we can't do this. We're both on the witness list."

"If you hadn't, I wouldn't have found the car or the boat or the sunglasses on the boat. They would have been found eventually by somebody, I guess, but pointing me there got them found a lot sooner."

He was still smiling—the smile hadn't faded since he'd greeted me in the reception area—but the voice behind the smile was hard.

"I thought this was about the job," he said.

"It is about the job."

"But we're not talking about the job."

"Maybe we are talking about the job."

"So it's about the job?"

"The DA has a problem," I said. "A hole in their theory. Tom dispatches Katrina, throws the body into the trunk, drives all afternoon to Savannah, loads her on the boat, and dumps her a hundred miles offshore. He gets back before his first class the next morning at ten—but how? How does he get back to Knoxville if he leaves the car on Tybee Island? He didn't rent one there and he didn't fly, so how did he get home?"

"Maybe he hitchhiked."

"Right. Or maybe he's applied his mathematical genius to inventing a teleportation machine. Or maybe, just maybe, he had an accomplice."

"Who followed him down to Tybee and drove him back."

"Nobody's asked me how I knew to look for her in Savannah. Yet."

"Somebody ought to talk to the girlfriend," Dresden Falks said. "She'd be my bet."

"Because you have an iron-clad alibi."

"Jeez, Ted, I do something like that and I could lose my license. Can't practice detection without one, you know. Oh, wait."

"Only reason I'm here today, Dres. The well's running dry."

"Gotcha."

"And I wouldn't want to walk into a situation on a basis of distrust. Did you help him that day or did he tell you after the fact?"

"Neither."

"So why did you say she was in Savannah?"

"Um. Lucky guess?"

"You think the DA will buy that?"

"I don't give a flying fuck what the DA buys. Look, Ruzak, you called me, wanting to talk about a job, and so far you haven't said word one."

"Maybe I'm trying to demonstrate what a hard-case tough guy I am."

"I'm underwhelmed. You want to know what my testimony will be? I'll tell you what my fucking testimony will be. Tom Bates hired me to get that case file from you, which I did and which, in turn, I gave to him."

"That can't be it."

"Why not?"

"Not all of it. Like I said, the DA hasn't asked and I don't know if he will, but you can bet your trophies over there that the defense will, and I'm not going to perjure myself, Dres. I'm not risking jail time for some obnoxious George Clooney clone with delusions he's living in a Mickey Spillane novel."

Oh, that smile. Maybe he put it on the mornings, between polishing his shoes and knotting his Armani tic.

"Tom Bates offered me half a million dollars to off his wife."

"I don't believe that."

"How come?"

"Because you'd take it."

"That wounds my feelings, Ted."

"That presupposes you have them, Dres."

"He had it all figured perfectly, like one of his goddamned theorems."

"Proofs," I said.

"Huh?"

"Never mind."

"Snatch her in the middle of the night, take her over to the island, and dump her in the Atlantic. Said the affair actually worked to his advantage, gave some cred to her just taking off, that, plus, there's a pattern of her doing it. I told him no, laughed it off, sure he was just blowing hot air . . . until the bitch actually went missing. I figured the stupid fuck did it or found somebody else to do it, and most likely he stuck to his original plan."

"He came to you with this after he got the case file?"

"Yep."

"What was he looking for in that file?"

"Hell if I know."

"Did he think she was having an affair?"

"I don't think he cared."

"Then why kill her?"

"Ask me, I'd say he just didn't like her. You know what that sick fuck did? This was before you even came into the picture. He had me take some pictures of him with his little girlfriend and mail them to his wife."

"I think I've seen those pictures."

"Then enter Theodore Ruzak. Tom calls me up, says, 'My wife's hired this dorky detective; find out what he knows.' I say, 'What's it worth what he knows?' You know the rest. A couple days later, he comes back to me and says, 'I want you to make my old lady disappear.'"

"There was a lie in the file," I confessed. "He must have taken it to mean she was cheating on him."

"A lie in the file?"

"The reasons seemed valid at the time."

"Most reasons do. I guess the point here, Mr. Hard Case Tough Guy, is you really got no leverage. I got nothing to hide. I'm the DA's fucking star witness."

"There's something else," I said.

"Always is."

"About the pictures."

"What about the pictures?"

"Why did Katrina Bates hire me to prove something she already had proof of?"

"Maybe it's like somebody with a fatal disease. You know, getting that second opinion."

"Or she wanted him followed for a different reason, something having nothing to do with an affair."

"Like what kind of reason?"

"The same reason he wanted the case file."

"You know what I think, Ted? I think you're worryin' this thing like a dog with a bone. You're making it way too complex. This is your basic domestic homicide, with a little pussy on the side."

"Maybe he talked to someone else about killing her, and he was afraid I'd turn up that somebody else."

"Except he didn't talk to me about it till *after* he had the file and *after* she hired you."

"Doesn't mean she didn't suspect something before."

"Gnaw, gnaw, gnaw. Look, we both know he did it, and here you are nibbling around the edges like it amounts to a hill of beans. The important thing is they got him."

"No," I said. "The important thing is she's dead."

SCENE TWO
Market Square Diner

An Hour Later

Called your bluff," Felicia said. For some reason, she had dyed her hair platinum blond and gotten a French manicure, like she was auditioning for the lead role in a Madonna biopic. She had changed her perfume, too, from something musky to more flowery.

"More a feint than a bluff," I said. "I figured it would give me some cred, the seedy quid pro quo angle."

"'Cred'?"

"Dres used it. I'm susceptible to others' verbal tics."

"The feint or bluff, or whatever you want to call it, before this one may have gotten your client killed," Felicia said. She was talking about "K.B. having illicit liaison with BF." "Never play poker, Ruzak."

"I always hated card games," I said. "Every Saturday night, my parents forced me to play euchre, and it was torture."

"Tommy loves Uno."

"Played that, too. Hate it worse than euchre. It's spiteful."

She laughed, for some reason.

"See the paper yet?" She dropped the front section beside my plate of scrambled eggs. "Tom Bates made bail. Two point two million dollars."

"He looks drawn."

"Facing capital murder charges will do that to you."

"Dres picked him up in Savannah," I said. "He suggested it was Kinsey, but that just feels wrong."

"Feelings. Ruzak, it was your feelings that landed you hip-deep in this mess in the first place."

"Right, and those pesky feelings led to justice for Katrina."

"Sounds like the perfect title for the based-on-a-true-story TV movie: *Justice for Katrina*. Maybe that should be your new career path. You could write and star in it as yourself."

"She might fess up," I said, meaning Kinsey. "If it was her, if they offer her immunity."

"Maybe they have. They don't include you in the strategy sessions, Ruzak."

"Here's the thing: If I have these niggling questions, won't the jury? Here you have a guy from the best family, with superlative genes, everything to lose, very little to gain, who looks good and talks good and could charm the socks right off my spinster aunt Regina, who's never been arrested for so much as jaywalking, who gives millions every year to St. Jude's Hospital, for Christ's sake, and they're supposed to believe he murdered his wife over the very thing he was doing himself? Had *been doing* himself since day one of the marriage?"

"Men are hypocritical assholes," she said, but she said it with a smile. "I bet you the prosecution packs the jury with women."

"Could backfire," I said. "This guy's got a way with the ladies."

She sipped her green tea. I sipped my black coffee. Sunlight glistened on the ends of her newly minted hair.

"Did you see the sign next door?" she asked. "Prime office space, Teddy. You'd be sandwiched between here and the noodle place. It's perfect."

"We'd need a new name." I was being semiserious.

"Teddy Ruzak, Inc."

"Nothing with my name on it. Too sniffable."

"'Sniffable'?"

"How about Carpet Land, and we put samples on the floor to make it seem legit."

"What happens when people come to buy carpet?"

"We sell it to them."

"Ruzak, you'd be a horrible salesman."

"Didn't stop my dad."

"You're too honest."

"That's the irony. When I chose not to be, somebody paid with their life."

"You don't know that for sure."

"For sure all I know for sure is I don't know anything for sure."

"If that's a quote, you owe me a dollar."

"Paraphrase—not covered by the rules."

SCENE THREE
Apartment

Fourteen Hours Later

A rchie began barking before the banging even started—a good thirty seconds before—clawing at the door of his crate as I stumbled toward the door of mine. "Archie, stop!" *Bang-bang.* "Archie, stop!" *Bang-bang.* I put my eye to the peephole and through it saw the last person I expected to see. I threw back the bolt, opened the door, and he stumbled into the room, reeking of alcohol, wearing the same suit from the day before (I recognized it from the picture in the paper). He staggered toward the bar and said, "Ruzak, can I come in?"

"You are in," I said. I closed the door, threw the bolt. Archie whined, his thin tail a blur, and scratched at the bars of his prison. I let him out. He made a beeline to Tom Bates and commenced licking his hand.

"But you shouldn't be," I said. "If anyone knows you came here, we're both in deep do-do."

"No one knows. No one."

He heaved himself onto the chair at the bar and asked if I had anything to drink.

"Bud Light," I said.

"Jesus Christ!"

"I'd take you for a Heineken man."

"If it's all you have."

"Maybe you've had all you should have."

"Maybe you shouldn't worry about what I've had."

"I'm not worried about you at all," I said. I set a Bud Light in front of him and his Adam's apple jumped as he threw back his head and drank. With his left hand, he absently scratched behind Archie's ears.

"I like your dog," he said.

"I'm looking for a good home," I said. "But I don't think they allow pets on death row."

"I didn't kill my wife."

"Doesn't matter what I think, Mr. Bates."

"Tom, please."

"Tom, please . . . leave."

"I don't understand; I really don't. How things . . . This is so . . . Everything . . . In a nanosecond, everything can . . . Do you have another?" He waved the empty can in my face.

"Moot point," I said.

"She was a great fuck."

"Excuse me?"

"Katrina. My wife. Reason I married her. She had money, but I had more. She was pretty, but I'd had prettier. She was smart, but there were smarter ones. The thing she had, the one fucking thing—ha!—she could *fuck*—fuck your brains out; fuck you like she invented fucking. She was the da Vinci of fornication, the Mozart of screwing, the . . . the . . . Mark Twain of carnality."

"Mark Twain?"

"You know what I mean. You know. That's your ploy, your gig, your shtick, Ruzak. I saw it from the first, the very first time we met. It's all a fucking act with you, this air of befuddlement, like Hamlet with the players; you think I don't see through it?"

"If she was so great in bed, why did you fool around on her?"

"Her fault."

"Well, sure."

"No, it's the truth. It was like she set a fire and it raged until it ate up all the oxygen in the room. I'm monogamous by nature—why the hell do you think I stayed married for twenty fucking years?"

"I don't know the answer to that."

"I'll tell you the fucking answer to that. I loved her! How about that? I married her for sex, stayed married for love."

"Okay. So you didn't kill her. Who did?"

"I want another beer."

"Mine's not the only bar in town."

"May I have another beer, please?"

I handed him another beer.

"I don't know who killed her," he said. "I don't know shit. I don't know how her blood got in our kitchen or in the car. I don't know how the car got to Tybee and I don't know how the sunglasses got on the boat and I sure as fuck don't know what happened to my poker. My poker!" He laughed. "That's a good one."

"It isn't me you have to convince, Mr. Bates."

"It's a start. All the great religions, they started with convincing just one person. Go back further, Ruzak; go back to prehistory. Some caveman had to convince another caveman if you sharpen a stick and throw it at the fucking mammoth, you might just be able to take down the big hairy son of a bitch. Go back even further. Some slimy vertebrate had to convince another slimy vertebrate to come out of the water, that the beach was fine. You get it. You're not dumb."

"No. Just confused, which is often mistaken for dumbness in slimy vertebrates."

"I was resigned to it, the divorce. Resigned, as in tired of the whole damn thing. All the hysterics, the theatrics, the melodramatics. Maybe you didn't know her that well, but Kat knew how to play the part. Jesus shit, she *loved* the part, the wronged woman, the long-suffering wife to the wandering Lothario. She told everybody who'd listen. We'd be at a faculty party and she'd turn to someone we barely knew and say, 'Tom screws around.' Or something to that effect. 'Tom can't keep his dick in his pants.'"

"Twenty years of that could build up some real resentment."

"Okay, I see where you're going. It's so offensive. Really, I mean, look at me, look what I've done with my life, look at my reputation. I came *this* close to a Nobel. Did you know that? *This close.* And I was forty-one years old, Ruzak. Forty-fucking-one!"

"That's your defense?" I asked, unable to help myself. "You're too smart to have done it?"

"Too smart not to cover it up a little bit better, for Chrissakes. Blood splatter on the kitchen cabinets, Ruzak? Tossing the poker instead of cleaning it and putting it back? Dumping the car in a place where someone was sure to find it? I ask you honestly! Is that the behavior of a man of my intellect?"

"The prosecution's theory," I said slowly, "as I understand it, is you blew up that afternoon, killed her in a jealous rage, and got sloppy in your haste to cover it up."

"Okay, but I had *weeks* to make sure I'd dotted all the *i*'s and crossed all the *t*'s."

"You tossed the poker somewhere where it couldn't be retrieved—say into the ocean with your wife's body. The sunglasses fell off as you heaved her over the side; it was the dead of night; you missed them in the dark. You left the car there because where else would you leave it? Just a plausible *she* left it there and took off with a third party, easily explained, at least easier to explain than if some fisherman hooked it in Lake Loudon."

"And the blood? What about the blood?"

"Very small specks, as I understand it. You cleaned up the worst and didn't see the rest on the dark paneling."

"Ah." He waved his hand dismissively, a professor to a thick pupil. "Crap."

"Why did you refuse a polygraph if you're innocent?"

"Because I'm a scientist and that's not science. Besides, my attorney said he'd cut off my balls if I took it."

"And you're gonna need those."

He teared up. I had the sudden, nearly overwhelming urge to smash my fist into his face.

"Right at the cusp, Ruzak. At the very brink of it. Like Moses on the mountaintop. I was going to start my life anew. I was going to have everything, everything that bitch denied me."

"Children," I said.

He hit the countertop with his fist and then literally fell off his stool. Archie beat a quick retreat before getting squashed. I pulled Tom Bates from the floor and he collapsed into my body, pressing his face into the crook of my neck, where I felt his tears against my skin, which was crawling by this point. I pushed forward as he pressed back, his hands gripping my shoulders.

"I wanted a son, all I wanted . . . all I wanted!" he sobbed. I eased him backward toward the sofa, thinking, *Who's the hysterical one now?* His feet shuffled on the hardwood between my bowed legs, as if we were engaged in some weird, vaguely Eastern European folk dance.

"And she knew it. She *knew* it was the one thing. The one thing that would hurt me the most. She could have given me that, she could have, and if she had, she wouldn't be dead."

He felt the sofa with the back of his legs and let go, one arm thrown over his eyes, the other dangling over the edge. Archie eased up and gave his knuckles a tentative lick.

"That's why you killed her?"

"I . . . didn't . . . kill . . . her."

"See, this is where intelligence can whip around and bite you, Tom. You wouldn't confess to me. You know I'd testify to it at trial."

"That judge is a fucking moron. I should be in a cell, under a suicide watch."

"Stop it," I said. "You've already said too much. Now I've got to call the DA in the morning and tell him you said if she had given you a son, she'd still be alive."

"That's not a confession to murder. That's a statement of the inevitable. You think I would have jeopardized my marriage if I'd had a family?"

"Have kids, no Kinsey?"

"Kinsey," he moaned. "That's done now, no matter what happens."

"Was it her? Did she come over and help you clean up, follow you down to Tybee so you'd have a lift home?"

"That's what they think."

"Who?"

"The fucking DA's team, who do you think? I called her that afternoon. They pulled the records."

"And she came over."

"I asked her to come over. Not for any fucking cleanup operation. I just said, 'Hey, she isn't here; come on over and help me pack.' They offered her a deal. Immunity if she testified against me."

"She turned them down."

"She stayed with me that night. She's my alibi."

"Pretty weak one."

"And I'm hers."

"You're . . . hers?"

"Hers. Hers. I'm going to tell something now no one else knows, Ruzak, and you tell anyone, I'll deny it, understand? She's on the cop's side. She thinks I did it."

"Some alibi."

"Not because she saw anything or I told her anything. It just makes sense to her: I killed Katrina to get her out of the way, to keep her from taking everything in a divorce. That's what's so fucked. That's why I should be on suicide watch, why I'm drunk, and why I intend to stay drunk until this trial's over, whether I walk out the front doors or into the death chamber, because a couple months before Katrina goes missing, she finds out she's pregnant."

"Katrina was pregnant?"

"No, you obtuse son of a bitch. *Kinsey. Kinsey* was pregnant." His arm fell from his face, and I had never seen such complete despair as I saw in Tom Bates's eyes—not even in the eyes of my dying mother, for whom all hope of life had departed.

"With my son," he whispered. "My goddamned son, Ruzak! The one thing I wanted. The one thing. Would have traded all of it, down to my last stitch of clothing. That one thing. Yesterday, I go home to the scene of the crime—the scene of the crime!—and she isn't there, and I call and call and call, and when she finally answers, I ask her where she's been, told her I'd made bail, told her

I was home—*our* home—and she tells me then, she confesses then, she did it, she's the killer. She's the one who took it from me. First Katrina and then her. That one thing. That one thing. She's the fucking murderer, not me."

"She aborted the baby."

He wailed at the words. This time—I can't really give all my reasons—I held him while he cried. But *cried* really doesn't do it justice. This was the sound of a man's soul being ripped to shreds. *The only genuine tears we cry are for ourselves.* I wondered if I had read that somewhere or if it popped into my head wholly formed in all its profundity, like the goddess of wisdom exploding from the head of Zeus. Didn't matter.

SCENE FOUR
District Attorney's Office

Early the Next Morning

W ow," the man said. "That's weird."

Assistant DA Howard Beecham threw one cowboy-booted foot on top of his desk and leaned back in his chair, craning his neck to peer at me over the listing stacks of case files piled five or six high on the desktop, like a wary meerkat eyeing the terrain.

"The jury might not think so," Meredith Black said.

"Ah, the jury's gonna take one look at that girl and know she couldn't have—just not in her."

"Offer him a deal, Howard," Meredith said.

"No deal."

"I'll go to French." Martin French was the district attorney, Beecham's boss. Beecham gave a dismissive wave: *Go ahead to French; you're wasting your time.* "This changes things," she insisted. "If he was covering for her, he might be ready to change his mind."

"Where is he now? Where's Bates?"

"Asleep on my sofa," I said.

"You are walking a very thin line," Beecham said, aiming his index finger between the stacks and pointing at my face. "No more contact with Bates, understand?"

"He came to me."

"I'm gonna go to the judge and get his bail revoked," Beecham vowed.

"Maybe you should," I said. "He's unstable."

"Think so? Not what I think. Wanna know what I think? I think he's playing you for a fool, Ruzak. 'I didn't kill my wife. Boohoo.'"

"You wanna know what I think?" Meredith said. "I think you've got a bigger problem than Tom Bates crying to Ruzak about his wife."

"He didn't cry about his wife," I said. "He cried about his baby."

"Ah, come on, don't you get it, Howard? This is a gift," Meredith said. "They're going to use Kinsey to establish reasonable doubt."

"Well, Meredith, the defense always uses *something*."

"Right, and the something they're going to use is Ruzak."

"Ruzak?"

"If you don't bring up what happened last night on direct, you can bet they will on cross. They're gonna ask, 'Did the defendant state *he* was *her* alibi, Mr. Ruzak?' They're gonna ask, 'Did the defendant say, quote, *"She's* the one, *she's* the killer?"'"

"What I was saying. It's a game."

"It might be a setup," I said. "It might have been orchestrated, but why go to all the trouble? Why not just put Tom on the stand and have him tell the jury the same thing? Why have it come through me?"

"Which is why you go back to them and offer the deal," Meredith said. "No death penalty if he turns. Go to trial and you risk a hung jury or even an acquittal. Least this way, whether he's guilty of the murder or guilty of the cover-up, he pays."

Beecham didn't say anything for a minute, but he was smiling at us.

"This is bullshit," he said. "That girl didn't take a fireplace poker upside that lady's head. You know it; I know it; Christ, even Ruzak knows it. But here we sit, discussing it like it's a real possibility. Then you suggest I go to them and throw in the towel, like, Jesus Christ, there's no way we can overcome this powerful 'my girlfriend did it and I covered for her because she was bearing my child' theory, so guess what? You win; we're throwing in the towel. . . . I'm not buying it, Meredith, and I'd bet my left nut the jury wouldn't, either."

She said, "I want to wire Ruzak."

"Huh?"

"I want Ruzak to wear a wire and talk to Kinsey Brock."

"And that's going to accomplish . . . what?"

"It wasn't just a fetus she aborted yesterday. She threw the whole thing overboard. She's got nothing and nobody to protect now—except herself. She might talk."

"But why Ruzak?"

"He's not law enforcement."

"That's my *point,* Meredith. Maybe *we* should talk to her to find out if she's ready to talk."

"That ignores the other possibility," I said. "Tom *is* playing some kind of game. You guys go to her and he'll know his bluff's been called. He'll know I came to you. I go and both of them might think the mark's bought the con."

He said, "'The mark'?"

"Me."

"Play the fool."

"I have some experience," I reminded him.

"It's a waste of time," he said.

"Oh, Howard," Meredith said. "What the hell do you have to lose?"

He thought for a long while about his answer.

SCENE FIVE
Sunsphere Observatory,
World's Fair Park

The Next Day

*T*he weather had turned humid, eighty degrees by midmorning; the leaves of the Bradford pears had fattened, the emerald green deepening to Celtic. Kids in bathing suits splashed in the reflecting pool, overseen by mothers with dabs of sunscreen on their noses. Somewhere out of sight, a lawn mower roared and spat. Summer was in full swing.

Kinsey Brock met me on the observation floor of the Sunsphere, wearing a midriff T-shirt and a pair of tight cargo shorts terminating two inches below her crotch. A diamond stud glittered in her belly button. No makeup besides a touch of lipstick. She was about a head shorter than I was. Though only about ten years separated us, I felt like a father escorting his daughter on a field trip.

"Wow," she said. "I've never been up here."

"You a native, or just going to school here?" I asked.

"Oh, I graduated last spring."

Not an answer, really, and spoken softly, so whispery, I was afraid the mike wouldn't pick it up. I eased closer to her as she leaned over the wooden rail to look straight down to the park beneath us. Not father now. Molester. I was wearing a windbreaker to help hide the wire, overdressed for the heat.

"Thanks for talking," I said.

"You sure it's okay?" she asked. "I don't want to get into trouble. Any more trouble."

"Not your fault, right?"

"Not his, either. I know you don't believe that. You're on the other side."

"I'm on nobody's side."

"You were on Katrina's."

"I guess if I'm on anyone's side, it's the truth's."

"And the truth is, he didn't do it."

"If not him, who?"

"I don't know who. All I know is, he didn't. He didn't have time. And he didn't leave that night; he didn't go anywhere. I was there the whole time with him. I know."

"Maybe somebody else took the car over to Tybee."

"Well, somebody else had to, because it wasn't Tom."

"You know Dresden Falks?"

She shook her head. Now she was looking west, into the hazy sprawl of the interstate and the attendant strip malls and low-cost apartments. I smelled bubble gum.

"He's a PI," I said.

"I thought you were a PI," she said.

"He's Tom's PI," I said.

Blank look. I said, "Dresses like an investment banker. Looks like George Clooney. The actor. Um, *Oceans Eleven, Michael Clayton.*"

She shrugged. "I don't know everybody Tom knows."

"I think you've met. He's the guy who took the pictures."

"What pictures?"

My face grew warm. "The pictures of you and Tom doing, um . . . Being intimate. Together."

"Nobody ever did that. Why do you think somebody did that?"

"I saw the pictures."

"Oh."

"Commissioned by Tom."

"He would never do something like that."

"And mailed to Katrina."

"By Tom?"

"So you didn't know anything about that?"

"Of course not."

"He must have been hiding somewhere, maybe the closet."

"Where are the pictures? Can I see them?"

"Not now, but you will. In court."

"They're going to show them in court? Oh my God."

"They establish motive."

"What motive?"

"You, Kinsey. You're the motive."

She shook her head again. "I'm not the motive. What I got rid of two days ago, maybe, but not me."

"Well, that's why I wanted to talk to you. About what you did."

"I can't believe he told you. It's none of anybody's business."

"You know, some people might look at what you did as a . . . well, as a kind of admission of something."

"Like he's guilty or something?"

"Like that."

"But he isn't guilty. I know he isn't guilty."

"So why aren't you standing by your man?"

"He isn't 'my man,' Mr. Ruzak. He knew what I was going to do before she even disappeared. I'm twenty-three years old. I'm not ready to have a kid."

"Tom sure was. You two didn't have any plans to get married?"

"Oh, we talked about it. But I'm twenty-three years old. I'm not ready to get married."

"If that was the plan, why did you wait till the eve of his murder trial to have an abortion?"

"Can you think of a better reason?"

"So it's over."

She nodded. "Over," she whispered.

"'Hell hath no fury like a woman scorned,' Kinsey, but men are a close second."

"What's that mean?"

"It means there's a pretty good chance Tom is going to use you. He's going to get even. He's going to suggest that you killed Katrina."

She looked at me as if I had just sprouted a second head.

"Because she was in the way, going to take all his money. This meddlesome, hyperkinetic, obsessed older woman with a penchant for melodrama was stopping your ride into the sunset with the father of your child. You know, it isn't inconceivable; it could have happened. Tom calls you, says, 'Meet me at my place. I gotta get some things.' You show; he's not there yet. But Katrina is, and maybe she loses it. Maybe you were just protecting yourself and your unborn child. What choice did she give you? Then it's like one of those things that there's no taking back, no do-overs; it's done and you have to deal with it. Tom shows up, and of course he's going to help you deal with it, because there's the baby to think about, too, an innocent life to protect, not that yours is chopped liver, but it's the one thing—that's what he told me two nights ago—it's the one thing that matters. More than Katrina, certainly, and probably a little more than you. You did what you did and now the thing that has to be done has to be done."

With gargantuan effort, I stopped myself. I could imagine Meredith and Howard's reaction: *Jesus Christ, Ruzak, you were supposed to tape* her!

"You're right about one thing," she said. "It was the only thing that mattered to him."

"So it makes sense."

She shrugged. We began to walk the circuit around the sphere. There was the campus and the football stadium. There was the boathouse and the river. There was Baptist Hospital on the bluff.

"You know what's funny, Mr. Ruzak?"

"What? What's funny, Kinsey?"

"Wherever she is, she must be laughing her ass off."

"Katrina? Why?"

"That's what I thought when I was on the table at the clinic. Thinking about her. How funny she would think it was."

"She knew you were pregnant?"

"I don't know. I'm talking about the abortion. She knew how much Tom wanted kids. It was like a vicious circle, you know? He cheated, so she refused; she refused, so he cheated. She would have *loved* it that I did what I did. Baby's gone, I'm gone, he's going to jail, and her dad's taking all his money."

"Her dad's doing what?"

"Tom said Alistair called him and said once the trial was over, however it came out, he was filing a wrongful-death case against him."

"That would just about cover it," I said. "That would be everything."

And here I had been thinking that irony was dead.

SCENE SIX
The Street

A Few Minutes Later

I loitered in the park for ten minutes, until I was sure Kinsey Brock was long gone, then went to the white van parked illegally next to the fire hydrant on the curb. I rapped on the door. It slid open and Meredith Black stepped onto the curb and stood next to me.

"Snake eyes," she said.

"Still worth the roll."

"Howard is never going to let me live this down."

"You never know. It's like gardening."

"What's like gardening?"

"The seeds you plant need time to grow. She's been through a heck of a lot over the past few months. Pregnant. Boyfriend arrested for murder. Abortion. She's in shock. She thinks about it for a few days, she might come clean."

"Unless she already has."

"That's her seed. Maybe he has, too."

"Come again?"

"I'm out of money. I guess you know the state's shut me down again. They took my files and warned off my clients and confiscated the entire contents of my office, down to the staples and my Starbucks coffee. I went looking for a job, but I brought the wrong dice to the table. I need bigger dice."

She gave a little laugh. "Ruzak, sometimes I have no clue what you're talking about."

SCENE SEVEN
Hilton Hotel Parking Lot

Three Days Later

Felicia pulled into a spot with empty spaces on either side and cut the engine. I checked my watch. Nine-thirty. I unbuckled my safety belt, loosened my tie, pulled on my collar, checked my watch again, asked Felicia to roll down the windows—it was a muggy, breezeless night—pulled down the visor, examined my teeth in the mirror, and looked at my watch.

"You're sweating," she said.

"Where's my gun?"

"I have no idea where your gun is."

"Here it is; I'm sitting on it."

"Basic firearm safety, Ruzak: Don't sit on your gun."

"I need to invest in a shoulder holster."

"Why?"

I pulled the flask from my jacket pocket and, grimacing, forced myself to swallow. Three quick ones. Felicia looked away. I looked at my watch.

"There's got to be an easier way to retire," she said.

"Both birds stone-cold dead this way," I said. "And if you're gonna go through all the trouble of saving somebody, you might as well make some money at it. . . ."

"Teddy Ruzak: savior for hire."

I ignored her. "How's it sound?"

She was staring straight ahead at the blank concrete wall, both hands gripping the steering wheel.

"Sounds good."

I looked at my watch.

"Stop looking at your watch."

I sipped from the flask.

"Go easy on that," she said.

"My last shot," I said, not intending the pun. "Last one."

"You look terrible," she said.

"Thanks."

"And you smell bad."

"Fetid," I said. "Bottom of the well."

"Barrel. Barrel is the expression. What about the cops?"

"That's gonna be tough. They like what they have."

"You don't."

"I don't have anything. That's the point."

"No. You don't like what *they* have."

"I don't have to like it."

"As long as you take advantage of it."

"Ever since I hung my shingle," I said, "you've been making re-marks, subtle and not so subtle, about how I need to toughen up, how I don't fit the hard-case, seedy PI ideal. This puts me there. See? I'm disheveled, I'm drunk, and tonight I walk through the final, dark doorway. Tonight, I'm thoroughly corrupt."

"You may have the seedy shtick, but you're still missing the li-cense."

"We could always take the act to another town. Another state even. How about California? It's a big state; we could go all Chandler with it. It would take awhile for anyone to figure the score."

"Did you just say 'figure the score'?" She was smiling.

"You know, I've never told you this, but ever since I first saw you at the diner, I've loved the way your nose crinkles when you smile."

"You've had too much. Give up the flask, Ruzak."

"It's my flask and you can't have it."

"You never talk this way."

"You've never seen me drunk."

"Are you drunk?"

"I'll shoot you," I said. "Try to take my flask and I will pull my gun out of my pants and shoot you."

Smile . . . and crinkle. *Maybe I should kiss her. Who knew what might happen up in that hotel room? I should kiss her. That's what any self-respecting hard-case gumshoe would do: give his gal Friday a passionate kiss before striding Gary Cooper–like toward his* High Noon.

"Seriously," she said. "No more. You don't want to walk in there totally witless."

"I'm not worried about walking in. It's the walking out I'm worried about."

I looked at my watch: 9:48.

"I have to go," I said. But didn't.

"I guess it's totally out of the question, my going with you."

I looked over at her. She was still staring at the wall, hands on the wheel.

"Wouldn't look right," I said. "Hard to explain. They'll understand me. Won't understand you."

"Who understands you?" she asked.

"They do. That's why this will work."

"You *hope*."

"I have to go."

"Okay. Tuck in your shirt."

"No."

"Don't get shot."

"Yes."

I got out of the car. "Roll up the windows."

"It's hot," she said.

"He might park in here. I don't want him to see you."

"Okay, but I'm leaving them down a crack."

I leaned in the open door. She finally moved her eyes from the wall to my face.

"What?" she whispered.

"That nose thing. The truth is, I just noticed it, just tonight."

I closed the door and repositioned the gun; the muzzle was poking into my butt bone. I walked away without looking back, trudging up the incline of the covered walkway to the front doors. The contents of the flask sloshed in my jacket pocket. I looked at my watch.

The elevator walls were mirrored, even the doors; I couldn't help but look at myself, unless I wanted to ride with my eyes closed, which would make the vertigo worse. She had been right: I looked terrible. I looked about as bad as Tom Bates looked the night he showed up on my doorstep and picked up where he'd left off, that insidious plot to steal my dog's affections from me.

In the hall on the nineteenth floor, I took one last look at my watch before knocking on the door. A couple minutes early, but heck, I was anxious. A woman called from the other side, "Who is it?"

"Me," I said. "Ruzak."

She opened the door.

SCENE EIGHT
Room 1921

A Few Seconds Later

S he was wearing a red silky kimonolike wrap over a blue one-piece bathing suit, blond hair pulled into a tight bun, and no makeup. He was looking fabulously fit in a yellow short-sleeve polo shirt and khakis. If either were taken aback by my appearance, neither showed it.

"So good to see you again," Anna Lynch said.

"Welcome to Knoxville," I said. "How was your flight?"

"Absolutely uneventful, but just in case, I heeded your advice and didn't order coffee."

"Well, I hear it's always smoother in first class."

"Mr. Ruzak," Alistair Lynch said. We shook hands. He was wearing a pair of reading glasses and holding a copy of the *Sentinel*. BATES TRIAL BEGINS TOMORROW blared the front-page headline.

I wet my lips. "Hey. Thanks for seeing me."

"You said it was urgent."

"You bet."

I cast a sideways glance at Anna, who was standing just outside my personal space with as prim an expression as you can muster in a low-cut bathing suit.

"We need to talk," I said to Alistair.

"Let's go down to the bar," he said.

"No," Anna and I said at the same time. Then she said, "I'm going for a swim."

"You said you changed your mind about a swim," he said.

"I changed it again," she said.

She left. Lynch sat at the small table situated three feet from the minibar. I sat on the foot of the king-size bed. He removed his reading glasses and laid them on top of the newspaper. He folded his hands in his lap and calmly watched me rub my hands nervously up and down my thighs.

"Thanks for seeing me," I said again.

"Are you feeling all right, Mr. Ruzak? You don't look well."

"I could use something to drink."

He gave a patrician wave toward the minibar.

"Help yourself."

I did—to the little bottle of Jack Daniel's. I poured it into a tumbler and knocked it back in a single swallow. My throat burned and my eyes watered.

"That's better," I said. "Thanks for seeing me, Mr. Lynch. I really appreciate it." It came out *appree-chate*.

"You said you had something important to tell me. About my daughter."

"Right, and I wouldn't bother you about any of this, because, A, we're both witnesses against Tom and we shouldn't be talking and, B, it's not so much about your daughter as it is about me and my current situation."

"Your current situation."

"Current situation, which is not good. I'll be honest with you,

Mr. Lynch. It's not good at all. *Not good* is too mild. *Sucks* is better.
I kind of left you with a false impression last time we talked, being
the fact that I'm a PI, which isn't a fact at all, but the opposite of
a fact, by which I mean a lie. I'm not a PI, I don't have clients, I
don't have an office—I don't have even have staples—and, more to
the point, I don't have a license. I never had a license. I didn't have
a license when I met you, I didn't have a license when your daughter hired, then fired me, and I don't have a license now. I don't
have much of anything now. Being a phony PI was my sole source
of income."

"I see."

"And this is my bad timing: At the same time I lose my business, the economy goes sour, leaving not just me but this very nice
girl who happened to take a chance on me and my cockamamie
idea to be a detective up the creek without a paddle."

"Mr. Ruzak, are you asking me for a loan?"

"God no. I'm not that creditworthy. Not that I'm a deadbeat.
Plus, you don't know me. We're practically strangers. If I was going to borrow money from somebody, it wouldn't be from somebody who couldn't be sure I could pay it back."

"I must confess, then, that I'm somewhat confused, Mr. Ruzak. How are your problems related to my daughter's death?"

"I didn't say they were. There's no connection at all. The state's
been after me since the get-go about this license, or lack thereof,
this crazy little Harry Truman look-alike who chases after me
like a bull terrier nipping at my heels, with court orders and search
warrants and whatnot, like I'm a mob kingpin or something, not
just some shmuck trying his best to eke out a meager buck for
helping people with their problems. Because that's all it boils
down to, Mr. Lynch. People, say, like you, enter into a contractual
agreement with people, for example, like me, to perform a service

beneficial to both. I help people out of their difficulties. I'm a helper. I'm Theodore Ruzak, helper for hire. That's how I saw myself anyway. Not somebody acting out a personal agenda or trying to take advantage of people. It wasn't like I was taking people's money and pocketing it without trying my utmost to help them solve their problems. I'm no con man or thief or vigilante, which I guess is Walter Hinton's take on me, but let me tell you, this guy is off his nut; he'd slap a fine on Batman and throw Robin in juvie hall. My point is, in my short tenure as a detective I've done more good than harm, helped more than hurt, added more light than darkness."

"You're one of the good guys."

"That's my perception, but the personal ones can be the most deceiving. I get that. I understand that. I try to be a straight shooter. I never cared for people who played games or got through life manipulating and using others. Never wanted to be that kind of person. Lately, though, I've been pushed further and further in that direction and really through no fault of my own. Take my dog."

"Take your dog?"

"I didn't mean literally take my dog. I mean I adopted this dog from the pound, thinking I needed a little companionship, but mostly it was like the PI work, you know, a mutually beneficial trade, because they would have destroyed this animal if I hadn't adopted him. It was down to the wire and I was his Hail Mary pass. So I take him in, but there's a prohibition against pets in my lease, and for the past couple of months the super has been all over my ass to evict him or me, or both of us, going so far as to break into my apartment while I was out and go through my things and, to be honest, deliberately trying to come between me and my dog. Steal his affections."

"Mr. Ruzak, are you drunk?"

"I am drunk. Yes, I am."

"I thought so."

"But I'm not rambling. This is important. I'm getting to it, but you need to understand the background, the context of my thinking. I have a point. I don't know if you watch much television, but I'm guilty of it, and not too long ago there was this news special about people who adopt monkeys not so much as pets, because there isn't much of a story there, but as surrogate children. Diaper them, take them to playgrounds, roll them around in baby strollers, plop 'em in the high chair for dinner. Refer to themselves as 'Mommy' or 'Daddy.' And inevitably it doesn't work out, because basically you can take the monkey out of the jungle, but you can never take the jungle out of the monkey. These monkeys are leopards whose spots will never change."

"The monkeys are leopards?"

"They'll turn on you every time."

"Good advice. Thank you. I shall steer clear of monkeys."

"Here's the point. The show's point. My point. It's all about connection. You know, when your daughter hired me, she said it wasn't about sex. 'This is not about sex' were practically her first words to me. Now on the surface, it *was* all about sex, about Tom fooling around on her since day one of their marriage, about a little twelve-year-old girl walking in on her beloved father with his wick dipped in the violin tutor. Sorry. Now it's one of your primal urges, right up there with eating, but there's another drive we're all prisoners to, another universal longing begging to be filled."

"Connection," he said.

"Right! The need to feel connected to someone, even if that someone is a fucking monkey—excuse me. We're so desperate for it, we'll turn to monkeys or, in my case, a dog who barely tolerates me. I think that's what Katrina was getting at. It wasn't—isn't—about sex. It never was. And Tom . . . I see you've got the paper there and I guess you know they revoked his bail."

He nodded slowly. I went on: "You know why he's on suicide watch? I do. The man who had everything—money, prominence, looks, women—in his heart had nothing because he didn't have a child. And he wasn't about to adopt a monkey and call himself 'Daddy.' Connection. Then at the very moment that connection he longed for was within his grasp, it was yanked away from him."

"You understand if I can't share your pity for Tom Bates, Mr. Ruzak."

"Well, I could pretend and say I hate the bastard, but I don't hate him, Mr. Lynch. Any more than I hate Katrina."

"Why would you hate Katrina?"

"Well, you gotta admit, it *is* a little beyond the pale."

"Yes. My daughter is the victim."

"That's the tragedy. They both are. Don't get me wrong. I'm not making excuses for him. He took certain vows when he got married and he broke those vows, but it just seems to me the punishment doesn't fit the crime."

"You don't believe murder justifies the ultimate punishment?"

"Oh, that's a whole other debate, Mr. Lynch. The Catholic side of me says you don't step into the shoes of God, and the Baptist side says hang 'em high. I understand you're filing a wrongful-death suit against him."

"Pending the outcome of this trial, yes."

"Well, that's why I'm here."

"You want me to share a portion of the proceeds with you?"

"How you finance it is completely up to you, Mr. Lynch. But hearing about it was sort of the final tip-off for me. It kind of set off this bell in my head, because I might not have the license, but

I kind of flatter myself that I have the instincts. I guess the first little bell was the pictures."

"The pictures?"

"In the box you held the key to. Pictures of Tom and his girlfriend doing—being unfaithful, on Tom's end. Those pictures were taken and that key mailed to you before Katrina hired me. In other words, she hired me to prove something she already knew. Why would she want proof for—of—something she already had incontrovertible evidence for—of?"

"I don't know the answer to that, Mr. Ruzak. And Katrina, of course, isn't around to provide one."

"You could extrapolate, like the prosecution: You know, Katrina disappears without a trace; we find her car on an island and her sunglasses on Tom's boat; there's blood all over the kitchen and car and boat, and trouble in the marriage. And of course the case file of a certain unlicensed PI hired by the victim to dig up some dirt on the accused, a case file the accused paid twenty thousand dollars to have. That's it in a nutshell, and you don't have to be a rocket scientist to connect the dots. You don't need a body to prove murder beyond a reasonable doubt. A body would be nice, and there've been cases where later they do wash up, but that won't happen in this case. You know it and I know it and one other witness for the prosecution knows it. The ironic thing is, the one person who doesn't know it is the person who's on trial for his life."

"I certainly do not know that. How do you?"

"I didn't, till yesterday. I don't know where your daughter is, Mr. Lynch. I'm not saying I do. But I do know where she *isn't*, or, more precisely, *what* she isn't, and that's dead."

He pursed his lips, stared hard at me. Then he stood up and said, "I think you had better leave."

"You haven't heard my proposition."

"I have no interest in hearing your proposition."

"I know it isn't all about money. I know it's mostly connection. Or the lack thereof. Your only child. The violin tutor. Her long-suffering mother. Not the tutor's, the child's. Guilt. Making amends. Maybe you bought in, thinking it wouldn't go this far, that there'd be no way they'd go for the death penalty in a circumstantial case. You might have gone in assuming the worst he could get was life. Or that the odds were, if it went to trial at all, he'd walk or there'd be a hung jury. Or maybe she played you for the fool, like she played me. And then, well, then there *is* the money, quite a lot of it if you win the case, and you need the money, Mr. Lynch."

"How would you know what I need?"

"The penthouse in New York is for sale, the house in Connecticut you sold last year, and the one in the Hamptons is in foreclosure. And your firm, Mr. Lynch, Lynch Investments, is in Chapter Eleven. You need the money."

"I have asked you to leave, Mr. Ruzak. . . ."

"My point is, it wasn't about sex; it was about destruction. And I knew that. I knew it the whole time. I had written it in the file: "Wants to destroy him.'"

There was a knock on the door. Neither of us moved.

"My wife is here," Alistair Lynch said. "I would prefer that you not be."

I looked at my watch. Right on time.

"It's not your wife," I said. "It's Dresden Falks."

SCENE NINE
Room 1921

A Moment Later

I stood up. Lynch didn't move.

"Who," he said, "is Dresden Falks?"

"I figured you'd want him here for this," I said. "So I took the liberty."

"I don't even know who he is," he fairly shouted at me.

I opened the door. Falks's thousand-megawatt smile faded when he saw Lynch.

"Ted," he said. "What's up?"

"Hey," I said. "Thanks for coming. We were just getting down to the nub of it."

I stepped aside for him to come in. He didn't. He stood in the doorway, smile dimmed to about forty watts; I could see the bottoms of his front teeth pressing into his lower lip.

"Ruzak," he said. "What are you doing?"

"What I should have been doing since day one, Dres. What everybody does because if they didn't, they wouldn't be, and if I had been from day one, I wouldn't have to be now."

"Huh?"

RICHARD YANCEY

"Looking out for numero uno. You really should come in."

He hesitated. He wasn't looking at Lynch now; he was looking at me, this Dresden Falks, who didn't need any lesson from me about who comes first. Finally, he stepped into the room, didn't speak for a second after I closed and latched the door, and then, as if some internal director had yelled *"Action,"* attacked the space between him and Lynch in four long strides, right hand extended.

"Dresden Falks. How are ya?"

Lynch folded his arms across his chest and said, "Mr. Ruzak, I have asked you to leave, politely, and now I must insist. You come here clearly drunk—"

"I am drunk."

"—babbling incoherently—"

"Okay, that's redundant."

"—making absurd allegations—"

"'Allegations'?" Falks asked. He was standing between us, head swiveling as we batted the ball back and forth.

"Oh, I have proof," I said.

"Proof of *what*?" Lynch demanded.

"What?" Falks echoed. "What proof, Ted?"

"I have to sit down," I said. I sat back down at the foot of the bed. The covers were still warm from my butt.

"This Polack won't tell me, but apparently you must know something about this, too," Lynch said, glaring at Falks.

"Hey, I don't know nothing except the Polack invited me here to discuss my client."

"That's it," I said. "Your client. His daughter."

Falks said, "His daughter isn't my client."

"Yes, she is."

"No, she isn't."

"Well. Not client maybe. Lover."

224

"Christ, Ruzak!"

"It's a guess, but an educated guess."

"I've had enough," Lynch said. He picked up the phone. "I'm calling the police."

"Don't do that," I said.

"Don't do that," Falks said.

"'Don't do that'?" Lynch asked.

Falks said, "What have you got, Ruzak? And if you got something, why haven't *you* called the cops?"

"He wants money," Lynch said.

"How much money?" Falks asked.

"We haven't gotten to that part yet," I said.

"He claims he's lost his business," Lynch said to Falks, but he wasn't looking at Falks; he was looking at me. Falks sank into the chair Lynch had occupied. There was another chair beside the table, but Lynch didn't take it. He was wound up. His cheeks were flushed; spittle shone on his lower lip.

"He did," Falks said. "Stupid shit came to me looking for a job."

"I'm out of sorts," I said. "Bottom of the well. Oh crap. *Barrel.*"

"Oh, this is rich," Dresden Falks said. "What are you selling, Ruzak?"

"A name."

"Whose name?"

"Katrina's."

Falks's smile broke the way the sun does at the beach at dawn: sudden, brilliant, hot.

Lynch exploded. "Bullshit!" he bellowed. "I don't know who the hell you think you are, coming into my room, trying to threaten me, blackmail me—"

"Uh-uh-uh-uh-uh," Falks said, holding up a hand. "Let's hear him out. This is interesting."

"My secretary, before she was my secretary, she was a waitress at the Old City Diner. You know the one? Not exactly the Four Seasons. A few years back, she was waitressing and going to school, studying to be a nurse, but she had to drop out when she got pregnant by a guy who ran out on her. She took a chance on me last year after my mom died and I came into a little money and started this business, and for a start-up we were doing pretty good, until the state shut me down over a minor technicality, and it's just about gone, all the venture capital and most of the money I made since then, and I feel for her, you know, and of course the kid, too, because he was a preemie and has some development issues. . . ."

"I can't believe this!" Lynch exclaimed.

"I could shoot him," Falks said pleasantly.

"That's a no," I said quickly. "No go, Dres."

"What did you mean, you want to sell Katrina's name?" Lynch said. He was going to wring it out of this goddamned Polack, so help him.

"Not her old name, obviously. Her new name."

Things got very quiet then. Falks didn't say anything. Lynch didn't say anything. In fact, the air drained a bit from his balloon. His shoulders relaxed. He blew out his cheeks. He sat in the empty chair opposite Falks, so now we were sitting in a kind of circle, though triangle would be more precise. We were triangulated.

"That's what I have," I went on. "And I want to be reasonable."

"This would be an excellent time for you to start," Lynch said.

"Katrina is alive," Falks said to me.

"Yeah."

"She faked her death."

"With help."

"My help?"

"Yes. Yours for sure. Mr. Lynch's here maybe, or after the fact."

"Why would she do something that like, Ruzak?"

"Well, I'm not in her head. She did tell me more than once that she wanted to destroy him. My guess, the deciding factor was Kinsey's pregnancy. I think that really pissed her off, which is kind of hypocritical when you think about it, not to pass judgment or anything. It might not have even been her idea originally. It might have been yours, Dres." I turned to Lynch. "It's back to that connection thing we were talking about. Dres needed Katrina and Katrina needed Dres. Dres wanted the money and Katrina wanted revenge. She also needed help with logistics, the planning and execution, setting up Tom and setting up a new identity—driver's license, birth certificate, passport, Social Security card. Maybe it's more than just a business relationship—that makes sense to my mind—since it's an awfully far way to stick out your neck, but Tom is worth an awful lot of money. So it could be just money, but it might be love, too. I don't like cynical people, so I struggle against my own. Not people, cynicism."

"You," Lynch said, "are a fool."

"Oh, you bet. I was played for one since day one. I wasn't hired to catch Tom; I was hired to create motive, or, more precisely, a file that Dres here could buy from me, pretending he was buying it for Tom. They didn't end up with quite what they wanted, so Katrina fired me and Dres made up the story about Tom asking him to make a hit on his wife. That morning, they staged the scene, and she called me to get the ball rolling. Why she chose me, I'm not really sure, except after my blowing the case file–setup thing, she figured she might as well try to recoup some of her losses. I didn't let her down, that's for sure: taking off to Tybee, finding the car and the glasses, going off half-cocked to New York to talk to you, Mr. Lynch, which worked out pretty good, saving you the trouble of contacting the authorities yourself and maybe setting off some warning bells. Looks better if the key evidence—no pun intended—came from the erstwhile amateur PI."

Lynch turned to Falks and said, "How much more of this am I expected to endure?"

"I'm liking it," Falks said. "It's pretty good. Ridiculous, but good." He smiled at me. "Like Ruzak. Okay, so your theory is Katrina Bates hires me to frame her husband for murder. . . ."

"Like I said, Dres, I'm not sure if it was that or something more personal. I do know the odds were good you two knew each other. He used you six years ago on a tail. Probably that's when you met her, or soon thereafter. It wouldn't be the first time a dick has fallen for the mark."

"Tom Bates hired me six years ago. True. Tom Bates hired me again six years later to take some pictures and buy a file from you. Also true. And true that Tom Bates tried to hire me to knock off his old lady. I'm Tom Bates's dick."

"No, Dres," I said patiently. "Tom Bates doesn't have a dick. You're her dick."

"I'm not her dick; *you're* her dick."

"My daughter has no dick," said Lynch.

"Like I said," I said, "maybe you were both, Dres. Her dick and her, um, dick. You followed her over to Tybee, where you dropped the car and planted the glasses, and then you drove her to the airport."

"Well, I see why you came to us instead of the cops. They'd laugh your fat ass right out the door. At least this gentleman's being a gentleman about it. If I were him, I'd pop you in the kisser for besmirching his daughter's good name."

"Which one?" I asked.

"That. Is. *Enough!*" Lynch said in a guttural monotone, forcing the words through his clenched teeth. "What do you want, Ruzak?"

"Oh God, I thought I was being uncircumspect about that at least."

"What a wise guy," said Falks. "What a cutup. Okay, big man, let's hear it. You say you have a name, give us a name. We're listening."

"I'd like to discuss price first."

"No money without a name."

"Something in the mid to high six figures." I was looking at Lynch. "Does that seem fair?"

"Why are you asking me?" he said.

"Because you're the banker. You fronted the twenty grand for the file and you're supporting Katrina until the big payout. Well, it would be more than a single big payout. You get a guilty verdict and I guess the insurance would pay out—not to Tom, but to her nearest living relative. So there's that on top of the wrongful-death judgment."

"Mr. Ruzak, I'm beginning to suspect you may be mentally ill."

"I'm drunk. I've lost everything I ever had, ever really wanted to have. Not that it was much, but it was mine, and, you know, I'm tired, damned tired, of swimming against the tide. Why should people like you and Deaddick Fuckhead here make out like bandits while my single-mom secretary with the handicapped kid and I suffer? You're not better than we are. You're probably not even that much smarter. I'm not sure; you might be, but I'm pretty sure Dres isn't. I'm sick of it, you want to know the truth, sick of people like him and Walter Hinton and Whittaker, that marplot, throwing their weight around like it *matters,* like it has any *meaning.* Life's not fair; that's what my old man always said. Or he'd snap at me when I complained, say, 'Hang on, lemme call the fairness police.'

It seems to me I can go on and be what I've always been, some-body's patsy, everybody's fool, or for once in my sorry little life I can stand up and demand a little of what's coming to me. I'm the one who followed it through. I'm the one who wouldn't let it go, and went to Tybee and found the sunglasses and tracked you down and finished it for you, did your dirty work for you, and now it's like I should be *grateful* that I don't have a fucking thing to show for it, excuse me, not a *fucking thing.* Well, no more. I'm getting what's mine, and what's mine is a prime number with lots and lots of zeros after it."

Dres Falks burst out laughing. He slapped his thigh. His shoulders shook with mirth.

"You play poker, Ruzak?" he asked after catching his breath.

"No."

"Good thing."

"Regina Giddens."

"What's that?"

"The name. Her name. Katrina's new name, the name she chose probably for luck and probably because it seemed to fit the situation so perfectly. Regina Giddens from *The Little Foxes.*"

Falks removed his handkerchief from his breast pocket and dabbed the corners of his eyes. Then two quick swipes across his nose and back neatly into the pocket.

"I'm impressed," Falks said.

"Shut up," Lynch said.

"No, for sure. Where'd you come up with that?"

"From me," Lynch said. His eyes were closed. "I told him."

It took a second for Falks to absorb that one.

"In New York, I was telling him about her first starring role," Lynch said. "Bragging about Katrina. But I *never* even *intimated* anything like what he's accusing us of."

"Another shot in the dark. Another bluff. When are you going to learn, Ruzak?" Falks asked. He had relaxed again.

"Regina Giddens boarded a Delta flight to Vancouver at the Savannah airport two days after Katrina Bates disappeared."

Falks was slowly shaking his head.

"And you know that."

"I do know that."

"How do you know that?"

"I have a friend down that way who has a friend who knows somebody with TSA. They checked the manifest. Regina Giddens, Delta flight one seven five eight, Vancouver by way of Atlanta. They faxed a copy to my friend."

"Let's see it," Falks said.

"Oh, Dres," I said, gently scolding.

"What does it prove, Mr. Ruzak?" Lynch demanded. "Even if someone by that name was on that flight, what does it prove?"

"It's the key," I said. "A key, like a theorem, doesn't have intrinsic value. The value of a key is what it unlocks. Like the one you gave me in New York. The name is the key and the key unlocks the box containing your daughter, Mr. Lynch."

He didn't get it. Dresden Falks did. He said, "The name gives you everything; it's just grunt work once you have the name. Passport and driver's license pictures, addresses, Social Security number, everything." He was eyeing me with a newfound measure of respect. *Ruzak, of all people, who would have thought?*

Lynch rose. Sat. Pursed his lips. Glared at Falks. Falks looked at him like *Hey, why you looking at me? You're the dumbass who gave him the name.* Then he looked back at me as I rubbed my thighs nervously, looking back at him with black-rimmed, reddened eyes, chin stubbly but thrust forward defiantly, a man holding a royal flush.

"How?" he asked finally.

"Hunch," I replied. "Cracker of some of the greatest crimes in history."

"A guess." He seemed incredulous.

"It was a long shot," I admitted.

"So's this," Dres said. He had commenced to cracking his knuckles, pushing his fingers back with the palm of his hand until the knuckles answered with a satisfying *pop*. I think I was supposed to think he was loosening up for a purpose.

"I didn't know," Lynch said. He wasn't looking at me; he was looking at the carpeting in front of my feet. "The name she chose. She didn't tell me, said it was best if I didn't know." He swung in Falks's direction. "*You* should have told me. If you had told me I never would have brought it up!" He turned back to me. "What is your price?"

"Okay," Dresden Falks said. *Pop! Pop!*

"Half a million dollars," I said.

"Okay, okay," Dresden Falks said. *Pop! Pop! Pop!*

"And an apology," I said. "For calling me a dumb Polack."

"I called you a Polack. No adjective."

"It was implied."

"Then I apologize for the inference."

"I mean, how would you like it if I called you an uptight, bigoted, morally bankrupt, sexually addicted, soulless, inbred WASP?"

"*Okay!*" Dresden Falks shouted, and came out of his chair. Now both men were standing about two feet from my spot at the end of the bed. "It's your money, Al, and far be it from me to tell you how to spend it, but he's taking you for a ride. He's gonna take the cash and still rat her out to the cops. Listen to me; I know this bozo. Thinks he's Jesus Christ come back to save the fucking planet, got a white-knight complex and he figures he can have his cake and eat it, too. There's no way on God's green earth he's going to let Tom Bates go down for this."

"Gee, Dres, that's flattering as all get-out. I had no idea you thought so highly of me."

He ignored me. His whole focus was on Lynch.

"There's no salvaging this if you say yes, understand? Say yes and we're all going down, you, me, and Katrina. This is serious shit, Lynch; this is serious time we're talking about. I've been there, done that, and bought the T-shirt. Al, you do *not* want to do time."

"What is the alternative?" Lynch asked.

"He wants to sell us his silence; I say we just take it."

Before anybody could move, the Luger was out of his shoulder holster and the muzzle jammed into the middle of my forehead.

"Don't be an idiot, Falks," Lynch said. "Put that away."

"This is a no-go," I said. "No-go."

"Why do you keep saying that?" Falks shouted in my face. Sweat was pouring from his and his hand was shaking. "Why do you keep fucking saying 'no-go, no-go' like that?"

The door shook violently on its hinges and an instant later splintered down the middle with an attendant thunderclap. Men in black body armor flooded into the room as I dived off the bed, fumbling for my .45 as I went down. The men were shouting, "Police! Get down. Get on the ground. Drop your weapon and get down *now*." I rolled onto my back, and there was Meredith Black, smiling, those long incisors bright lighthouse beams on a dark night at sea.

"I said 'no-go,'" I gasped.

"You were overruled," she said. "Mr. Ruzak." And she held out her hand.

SCENE TEN
The Office

Two Weeks Later

I mounted the stairs slowly, bearing the precious cargo: two large coffees balanced atop the box of Krispy Kremes. I stopped on the top step; a man stood on the landing, blocking my way. He was stenciling letters on the frosted glass of the door. WHITE KNIGHT ASS. He eyed the box.

"Let you in for one of those," he said.

"I gotta set the coffees down first," I said.

"How do I know you'll come back?"

I nodded toward the gold letters, still glimmering wet. "That's me."

He smiled. "Which part?"

"First part. Duty-bound."

Felicia was at her desk, talking to someone on the phone, and I did not envy the person on the other end. Felicia was not happy with their service.

"It's *knight, k-n-i-g-h-t,* as in King Arthur, the Round Table, Sir Galahad. Ever hear of them? Not *n-i-g-h-t . . .*"

I moved the coffees from the box to her desktop and went back to the stencil guy, who grabbed a doughnut from the box.

"Where's my coffee?" he joked.

Behind me, Felicia was saying, "Does that make sense to you, huh? *N-i-g-h-*t? 'White Night'? What kind of night is white? Alaska! What about Alaska? Are we in Alaska? Or are we in Knoxville freakin' Tennessee? . . . Oh, so now it's *my* fault I have three reams of stationery with the wrong name on it? Are you the boss? Where's the owner? I want to talk to the owner. . . ."

I grabbed one of the cups and a couple of doughnuts and went into my office, easing the door closed with my heel. I sat behind the desk, took that first exquisite bite, and chased it down with two sips of coffee.

The man in the visitor's chair said, "Mr. Ruzak, you've kept me waiting for over thirty minutes."

"Sorry," I said to Walter Hinton. "Wanna doughnut?"

"No, I do not want a doughnut."

"I didn't think so. You strike me as a Dunkin' man."

"This is all just a game to you, isn't it? You think it's funny."

"Maybe a little, in a creepy kind of pathetic way, like clowns are."

"Are you calling me a clown?"

"Be a little nuts if I did."

"Who is more clownlike, Mr. Ruzak? The licensing agent or the man who keeps changing his company's name, thinking that will fool the licensing agent? You can tell me the color of the sky is purple. That will not make it purple."

"Sometimes it is. At sunset."

"White knight," he sneered. "Let me ask you something, Mr. Ruzak. Who is going to ride to *your* rescue when I have you arrested for perjury and contempt of court? Just because you get your face on television and your name in the paper . . ."

"It's not my business," I said.

"Excuse me?"

"White Knight Associates. It's not my business."

As if we'd planned it, Felicia came into the room with a stack of papers and laid them on my blotter.

"Here's the incorporation papers," she said. "Sticky notes where you sign."

"Whose business is it?" Walter asked.

"Hers. She's the president; I'm the secretary slash treasurer."

She flashed a smile at him and sashayed from the room, perfume swirling in her wake.

"That doesn't matter," he said. "You can prop up a figurehead, but it won't change the basic fact that you are practicing detection without a license."

Cue Felicia. She came back carrying a hammer and something in a frame.

"Excuse me," she said, and commenced banging a nail into the wall next to my landscape of Cades Cove. She hung the frame, then stepped back.

"Does that look straight?" she asked.

"What is that?" Hinton demanded, but you could tell from his expression that he already knew.

"My license to practice private detection in the state of Tennessee," she said. She waved at me. I stood up and stepped to one side, and she slipped into my chair, folded her hands on top of the papers, and crinkled her nose at Walter Hinton.

"How may I help you?"

Hinton didn't answer. He stood up, got halfway to the door, came back, grabbed his briefcase, and then, back at the door, turned to us, opened his mouth like he was going to say something, closed it again, and then stomped out of the room.

Felicia said, "Exit Hinton huffily."

"I feel kind of bad for him," I said.

"For the love of God why?"

"All those hours wasted."

"It's his job, Ruzak."

"Can I have my chair back?"

"It's my chair now. If you're nice, I'll let you borrow it."

The phone rang. Neither of us moved to answer it.

"It's the phone," I said.

She nodded. "It's ringing."

"Are you going to . . ."

"I'm the president. Presidents don't answer the phone."

"I can't shake the feeling there's been this kind of coup."

"More like a power-sharing arrangement. Nobody's stopping you from taking the test again, Ruzak. Pass it and we'll reorganize."

"Meanwhile answer the damn phone?"

She laughed.

I answered the damn phone.

She didn't move from my chair—was it still my chair?—during the call. After the call, she vacated it and followed me into her office—was it still her office?—where the stencil man was putting the final touches on my ASS.

"Tell me again why you feel the need to talk to her," she said. "Falks cut a deal with Beecham."

I nodded. "Not Lynch, though."

"Lynch is a seventy-year-old man with connections. Connections that can fund his bond and keep the appeals going till he's six feet under. Lynch isn't going to cut a deal. He won't serve a single minute in prison for this."

"Maybe he shouldn't. He was played, just like everybody else."

"Ruzak, you don't walk a mile in somebody's shoes; you run a marathon."

"I don't like niggling questions."

"I didn't ask one."

"I mean Katrina's deal with Dres."

"And that matters because . . ."

"That's why I'm going to talk to her."

"And she would tell you now because . . ."

"She has a lot to lose."

"She'll just lie."

"For him?"

"For herself, Ruzak. She must be scared out of her mind."

"Why? Dres is locked up for the next fifteen years."

"Right. So what would be her reason to come clean with you?"

I thought about it.

"I guess it comes down to your basic outlook on humanity. That even Hitler might have been, if the circumstances had been different, reachable."

"Jesus," said the stencil man. "You *are* a white knight, aren't you?"

"That's the point," I said. "Because deep down I have this longing or hope that she's still savable."

"Oh, Ruzak," Felicia said. I sensed a metaphorical throwing up of her hands. She closed one eye, squinted through her thumb and index finger, lining up my head in the space between them, and then pinched her fingers tightly shut. "*Squish. Squish.*"

SCENE ELEVEN
The Hamilton

A Few Minutes Later

It was one of the newer condo buildings on Gay Street, across the street from the Tennessee Theatre, where two-bedroom lofts were going for a couple hundred thousand a pop. Hers took up half the ninth floor. The ride up seemed to take a long time, and I used that time to emit some serious flop sweat and worry myself with two conflicting hopes, one that I was right, the other that I was wrong. I usually worried, like most people, about being the latter. You don't normally hope you're wrong while at the same time being certain you're right. It would be like Jerry Falwell acknowledging the possibility of Vishnu in the cosmology.

"Hey," I said when she answered the door. "Thanks for seeing me."

The place was quintessentially lofty: sparkling new hardwood floors, windows every four feet or so with nice views of the city, open and echoey, with columns instead of walls for support. The furnishings were a little too modern for my taste, all sharp angles and shining chrome and bright Art Deco colors.

"I'm surprised," the woman who had called herself Regina Giddens said. "I figured the cops, not you."

"Are you asking if they know I'm here?"

"No."

"Well, they don't. Nobody knows. Well, my secretary and a guy we hired to put the new name on the door, but other than that, nobody."

"Not Dres?" she asked.

"No."

She sighed. I followed her into the main sitting area. The big-screen television in the corner was roughly the same square footage as my bedroom. She asked if I wanted a drink.

"Coffee would be nice. Black." I was trying to feel masculine.

I sat on the uncomfortable sofa with its one-inch cushions, sipping my barely palatable coffee—okay, maybe masculinity is not one of those things you can strain at—and she sat in the chair to my left, a contraption of canvas and metal that looked like a set piece from *Star Trek*. Not the classic *Star Trek*, *Star Trek: The Next Generation*.

"Thanks for seeing me," I said again.

"You're not wearing a wire, are you?"

"You could frisk me."

"I'd rather not."

"I'm not wired. Like I said, I'm here for me mostly, to dislodge some things that have been stuck in my craw."

"And I'm like the toothpick?"

"I'm guilty of the same thing sometimes," I said. "Stretching the metaphor until it snaps."

She nodded, like we were on the same wavelength. It hardly seemed possible, but she nodded, and pressed her knees together. Her knees were large, like the rest of her, including her best asset:

Her eyes were big and doelike, vulnerable, just a tinge of wistful-ness.

"There're some things I know and some things I don't know," I said. "That's pretty common, a universal malady, I guess. There're some things you don't know that I know and there are some things you know that I don't. That's why I wanted to talk to you. So I can tell you what I know and you can tell me what you know and then we'll both know what he knows."

"Everything that who knows?"

"Dresden Falks."

The big doe eyes cut away from my face.

"I don't know what he knows."

"But you know what you know."

"I don't know anything."

"Maybe we can start with what I know."

"Okay." She said it so softly, I could hardly hear her.

"You and Dresden Falks were lovers."

She drew a deep breath before answering.

"You don't know that."

"They do down at Velman."

"It wasn't like that."

"Wasn't like what?"

"We dated a couple times, that's all."

"Not what they say at Velman. The boss told me it ventured into the two-hour-lunch territory. Dres told me the street ran one way, a stalking situation, and he got you fired. But you weren't fired, Rachel. You quit. You quit two weeks before Katrina Bates went missing."

"Okay . . . so?"

"So that's the first thing I know. The second thing I know is that after you quit, you moved out of your apartment and into this

six-figure condo. A nice step up for an unemployed former receptionist."

"My personal finances are none of anybody's business, Mr. Ruzak."

She was putting up a tough front, but it really wasn't in this girl.
The eyes gave her away; the expression in them didn't jibe with
the severity of her tone.

"True. I guess you could have come into some money. A rich
relative died or you won the lottery. It's the timing that's trou-
blesome, Rachel. People around the office catch you and Dres
huddling behind closed doors; you abruptly quit; you move into
these posh digs. And then Katrina Bates vanishes off the face of
the earth."

"She didn't vanish. She flew to Vancouver."

"No, Regina Giddens flew to Vancouver."

"Well, Regina Giddens was really Katrina Bates."

"No," I said as gently as I could, and that took something. I
wasn't feeling too gentle. I was feeling pretty damned indignant.
"You were Regina Giddens."

She stood up. Dres had been unfair about her: She wasn't ugly.
As with a lot of big girls, that old saying about being pretty in the
face applied. Now that face was contorted with anger and maybe a
little bit of fear.

"Get out of here," she said.

"I will not."

"I'll call the cops."

"Hear me out. And after we're done, we'll go see them together."

"We are done."

"You haven't heard everything I know."

"You don't know anything. You're guessing."

"I know Regina Giddens boarded a flight to Vancouver from

Savannah. I know that after that she disappeared without a trace. I know the cops still can't find her and I know Dresden Falks is saying he doesn't know where she is, and *how could he not know where she is?* I know Regina Giddens didn't get on another plane and fly away and I know she didn't rent a car and drive away. You did. From the Avis at the airport. That was the mistake, Rachel. You flew up as Regina, but you came back as Rachel."

"Why would I do something like that?" she asked, eyes closed, as if steeling herself for my answer.

"You couldn't very well rent the car under the name of the woman who supposedly fled to Canada. For it to work for every-body—from Lynch to the cops—Regina Giddens had to fly there and stay there."

"This is . . . I don't know what . . . what you are talking about, Mr. Ruzak." Back to the wounded, confused, love-struck girl act, the words slamming into one another in a breathless rush. "She faked her death to frame her husband. You have that on tape. Dres *confessed*. I don't understand why you're here accusing me of these things. I didn't rent a car in Vancouver. Maybe *she* rented one using my name. Did you think of that? That would make sense, wouldn't it? Wouldn't that make sense, Mr. Ruzak? She switched identities again once she got there—"

"That's something I actually did think of," I said. "Once I got your name from the rental company. But it was a one-way rental, Rachel, Vancouver to Knoxville."

"So maybe she's back here in Knoxville."

I nodded. "Well, part of her is."

"Part—*part* of her?"

"They found her, Rachel. Most of her anyway. Two little boys hunting crabs on Tybee Island. This morning, they confirmed it through her dental records. Katrina Bates is dead."

She fell back into the *Star Trek* chair. She didn't have a choice; her knees gave out on her.

"I'll go with you," I said. "We'll go down to the station together."

"I didn't know," she said.

"No?"

"They dropped me off at the airport."

"Katrina and Dres."

She nodded. I pulled out my handkerchief and handed it to her. She didn't wipe her eyes; she wadded the handkerchief, worried it in her lap.

"They were going down to the island to stage the stuff in the car first, put the sunglasses on the boat."

"And then Katrina takes a later flight? But you were the one using the name Regina Giddens."

"She had another one, a different one. Name. She had a different name. I saw it."

"What was it?"

"I don't remember."

"You said you saw it."

"I did see it."

"Then what was it?"

"I don't remember! Dres showed it to me, passport, driver's license, Social Security card, everything. One set for me with Regina Giddens, another one for her."

"How did he sell it to Katrina?"

"He said I was the decoy."

"And she bought that?"

She shrugged. That did it. I shot up from the sofa. She shrank back in the chair.

"I want the truth," I said.

"I'm telling you the truth!"

"Katrina Bates was a lot of things," I said. "But one thing she wasn't was stupid. Why would she need a decoy? A decoy for what? Dres was her accomplice; why would she need somebody else to pull this off? She didn't; she wouldn't. But Dres did, didn't he? He needed somebody named Regina Giddens to sell it to the mark—"

"'Mark'?"

"The victim, the patsy, the fool, the mark of the con, Alistair Lynch. The cops had to believe Katrina was dead and Lynch had to believe she was alive. That was the only path, the only way to the money. And it's also the only explanation, Rachel, so stop playing around with me. I've been played like a Lynch a lot lately and I've taken a vow never to be played for one again. There weren't two phony names; there was just one. You know it. Katrina came up with the name, but Dres took it and you used it, like you knew before I even said it, just like you've always known it: Katrina Bates is dead. You were there. You saw it."

"I didn't see it!"

"Where did he kill her, Rachel? In the car, on the boat, in the beach house? Where did Katrina Bates die?"

She looked at me for a long, awful moment.

Then she looked away. "The water."

"The water?"

"He knocked her out on the boat and then we took the boat out and dumped her into the ocean with these two big concrete blocks tied to her ankles."

"She was alive when he dumped her over the side?"

"She woke up when she hit the water . . . and her hands came up, like this, and her eyes were open. . . ." Rachel Bisset's short, pudgy fingers clawed at my face on the ends of her outstretched arms.

"Okay," I said. "Okay." I lowered myself back onto the sofa, rubbed my face hard. "Okay."

We didn't speak for a few minutes. She sat in the chair with my handkerchief over her eyes and I sat on the sofa with the blinders off mine.

"So I was right—and I was wrong," I said finally. "She really is dead."

"You knew that already," she said without lowering the handkerchief. "You just told me they found her on the beach."

"No," I said. "Nobody's found her. I lied."

Now the handkerchief came down, a snotty little white curtain lowering.

"*Why?*"

"I was hoping I was wrong."

SCENE TWELVE
KPD Headquarters

Late That Afternoon

*M*eredith Black came out of the interrogation room and sat beside me.

"Well?" I asked.

"Oh, she's in love, she's in love, and she don't care who knows it. In the name of love. Blah, blah, blah."

"That word again," I said.

"You're not going all hard and cynical on me, are you, Ruzak?"

"I've been struggling lately," I admitted. "One of my core beliefs has always been in the basic goodness of people."

"Oh, there's a few of us out there, Teddy. I'm pretty good. And you're so good, you make good people look bad."

"You know who I was sitting here feeling sorry for?"

"Not her, I hope. She had her chance to save Katrina."

"Alistair Lynch. I'd hate to be the one who has to tell him she's dead."

"I'm not looking forward to it." She sighed. "But he *is* a greedy SOB; I'll try to keep that in mind."

"Katrina went to Dres first," I said. "That's how she got the pictures."

She nodded. "Right. And probably the whole 'Let's frame your husband' thing was his idea. It appealed to her sense of the dramatic, not to mention her vindictive streak, and she climbed aboard."

"And then he switches cars on her."

"He knew Tom was worth lots. But the really big bucks were out of reach unless Katrina was. So he played her. Played her dad. Played us. Tried to play you, but you don't play somebody like Theodore Ruzak. Too much openhearted dogged persistence. What was the tip-off?"

"Nobody could find Katrina. Lynch is arrested; Dres confesses; and still no sign of or word from Katrina. What did it mean? It stuck in my craw."

"I'm sorry, your . . . 'craw'?"

"There were only three possibilities, as I saw it. One: She switched identities once she landed in Vancouver, which would be pretty clever, a double-headed fake in case anyone stumbled across the Regina Giddens moniker."

"Which somebody did."

"Two: There was an accomplice waiting in Canada to negate any need of using the phony name. Or three: She was dead. I didn't want it to be three, didn't know where to start with one, so I decided to explore two."

"The accomplice angle."

"Right. The trouble was, where were they going to find somebody who would be willing to help?"

"Kind of payday we're talking about, wouldn't be too hard."

"Not based on the money, based on trust. Who could Dresden trust? So I started asking around Velman. About the receptionist who he said had a crush on him and the very weird fact that she happened to quit around the time Katrina disappeared. And they told me it wasn't a stalking situation like he made it out to be. Dres returned her affections. So I tracked down her address, found out she had moved recently from a four-hundred-dollar-a-month studio to one of the priciest condos in Knoxville. *That's it,* I'm thinking. *I found the accomplice.* I hit pay dirt at the car-rental place in Vancouver: Rachel Bisset booked a one-way rental to Knoxville forty-five minutes after Regina Giddens's flight touched down."

Meredith Black was smiling at me.

"And how did you get from that to murder one?"

"I couldn't think of any other explanation except that she was dead. No alternative theory could fit those facts."

"There's theory one: They flew up together and Katrina moved on under a different identity."

"What would be the reason? She needed a baby-sitter? And the salient point is her baby-sitter didn't stay to sit her. She came straight back to Knoxville."

"A third person met them."

"Too complicated. Every time you add a conspirator, it increases the risk of blowing the whole thing. And if a third person was waiting, why would Rachel need to fly up there?"

"You're short a theory, Teddy. Four: Maybe Rachel flew up to Vancouver a couple days before. To make arrangements prior to Katrina's arrival. Find her a hideout, buy her a cheap set of wheels, who knows? Katrina flies from Savannah as Regina, and Rachel is free to drive back home. Fits the facts perfectly."

"That could explain it," I said. "Which is one of the reasons I didn't go to you guys straight off with what I knew. There's a problem with it."

"What?"

"It doesn't rule out theory three."

"No. I guess it doesn't."

"See, I wasn't really out to prove any given theory was right. I wanted to prove that one theory wrong. And I knew if you guys contacted Rachel before I did, odds were she'd lawyer up or, faced with the evidence, might hook onto theory four and we'd never know the truth."

"The truth," she echoed.

"So I lied," I said.

"To get the truth."

"Not the usual door."

"The back door."

"Only door left unlocked."

"Because you wanted her to be alive," she said.

"I wanted to be wrong."

"And you really don't think you are about Lynch?"

"Oh, jeez, Meredith. His only daughter. Years of estrangement, short on cash, he was the linchpin—no pun—he was the key. She was doomed once her dad entered the picture, probably when Dres got the bright idea to kill her so all the money would come to him—it was all flowing to him anyway; he's already admitted to that."

"Still, Lynch could be lying. A man like him saying he wasn't allowed contact with her after the disappearance, that everything had to flow through Dres, it kind of stretches things."

"Maybe we're back to this cockamamie core belief of mine."

"How long could Dres reasonably stretch it out? That's my point."

"At least through Tom's trial. Probably even through the wrongful-death suit. It would compute. Why risk blowing the whole thing by contacting her? Lynch was sold because *she* was sold, and that's what gets me, Meredith, whatever your opinion of Katrina Bates; that's the thing that tears at me. When did it hit her? When did she know she was being played like she played everybody else? On the drive over to Tybee? On the boat, right before the hammer fell? Or—and this is the picture I can't get out of my head—did she not see it coming at all, and it was only after she hit the water and she reached for him, clawing at his shadow hanging over the surface . . . is *that* when it hit her? Is *that* when she knew?"

She didn't say anything. She put a hand on my forearm. We sat there and stared at the opposite wall, which was painted institutional beige. A big clock hung there, the small hand midway between the seven and the eight. It reminded me I hadn't had dinner.

"Wanna grab a bite to eat?" I asked.

"Give me a rain check," she said. "I have to take her down for processing."

"Pity," I said.

"I'm not blowing you off, promise. It's not you."

"Not me," I echoed. "Pity: It never would have occurred to me to check into the Rachel connection if I hadn't felt somewhat responsible for her losing her job. I don't think I even would have remembered the former receptionist he called 'a reject from the ugly factory.' But he made this joke, blaming it on me, on the fact that I had a pretty secretary and he didn't. So I felt sorry for her, this person I had never met, and pity made her plight stick in my craw."

"'Your craw must be pretty sore with so many things stuck in there." She gave my forearm a final pat and stood up. Her legs were long; the standing up took awhile. She was smiling down at me.

"I'll tell you what's the pity," she said. "I'm married."

SCENE THIRTEEN
The Sterchi Building

Late That Evening

You lied to me," Whittaker said.

"I've been wondering about this," I said. "Every time I see you, you're wearing the same suit or a nearly identical suit. Why is that? Is there a dress code or something? And doesn't that sort of demote you to a kind of glorified doorman or handyman?"

"Your thirty days have long expired, Mr. Ruzak."

"I have a proposition for you," I said. "Wednesday afternoons from five to seven, plus every other weekend. Two weeks during the summer. I'm responsible for a hundred percent of the upkeep, vet bills, medicine, food, toys, and incidentals."

"That isn't funny."

"I'll throw in alternating holidays."

"I could report you," he said. "Neglect. Animal cruelty."

"You're a tough negotiator, Whittaker. You take the nine-to-five shift, but I get him at night."

"I don't understand," he said. "Why don't you just give him to me?"

"Is that an offer?"

"I'm giving you the benefit of the doubt, Ruzak. Maybe you're having trouble finding him a good home."

"Which raises the question: Is yours?"

"You're considering it."

"Whittaker, I'm going to be honest with you."

"It's about time."

"This dog and I have had some bonding issues, some difficulties getting over the hump of establishing trust and intimacy. Sort of like an arranged marriage or taking in a foster child. In the ten months that we've known each other, that dog has yet to offer me the smallest smidgen of affection. Mostly, he stares. Sits across the room and stares at me like I have two heads. I've tried everything. I can't bribe it, trick it, or coerce it into loving me. But like any adoptive parent, I made a commitment to be in it for the long haul, and love is not an instantaneous big bang, but a tender seedling to be gently nurtured. Do you know, do you have any clue what it's like to bring a companion into your home, an animal not only renowned the world over for its unconditional acceptance and love but actually genetically engineered to that purpose over thousands of years, and have that animal reject you? It shakes you to your very core. It's worse than adopting a monkey; monkeys are wild animals with no history of domestication. It makes you question fundamental principles, long-held, psychologically stabilizing beliefs. It pulls up your anchor and sets you adrift in a sea of malaise. This animal, born and bred to love, loves everyone he meets— except me. Get it? It isn't the dog, Whittaker. It's me. If I give him up now, if I give *up* on him now, what does that say about me? That I'm unlovable even unto dogs? You see the dilemma."

"Maybe you haven't met the right dog." It was the best he could offer.

"Here's what you don't understand about me," I began.

RICHARD YANCEY

"I don't want to understand you," he said.

"I'm tenacious. I don't give up without a fight."

"Is that a threat?"

"Going into my apartment to verify compliance is one thing, Whittaker. Going into it over and over and over again to play with my dog is another."

"You can't prove that."

"Maybe I have video. Maybe I installed a nanny cam in his Yosemite Sam plushie."

"You don't give a crap about that dog. This is about beating me."

"That would make it about you. I just said it was about me."

Upstairs, I threw the dead bolt. From his bed across the room, Archie did not so much as raise his head. I had taken to leaving him out of the crate while I was at work, the guilt of locking him up outweighing the fear of him defecating on my sofa.

"Hey, Arch," I said. "Wanna go for a walk?" I jingled his leash. Nothing. I fixed his dinner and set it on the floor beside his water bowl. The sad brown eyes flicked back and forth, eyebrows went up and down; otherwise, nothing. I grabbed a Bud Light from the fridge and settled on the sofa. The afternoon sun shone through the open blinds, painting alternating bands of dark and light upon the hardwood.

My cell buzzed in my pocket. I didn't recognize the number. It wasn't Knoxville's area code.

"Ragman," purred the smoky voice of Melody Moy. "The famous Teddy Ruzak."

"Melody. Hey."

"Watcha doin'?"

"Nothing much. Playing with my dog."

"I didn't know you had a dog."

254

"Yes, you do. I told you."

"When?"

"At the beach house."

"You did?"

"And you told me you have a cat."

"I don't have a cat."

"You did but it died. Putin."

"Puffin."

"Okay, Putin is that Russian guy."

"What's your dog's name?" she asked.

"Archie."

"Does he have big soft brown puppy-dog eyes?"

"Oh," I said. "You bet he does."

"Guess what? I'm in the paper today."

"Really? That should help business."

"'Local Woman Key to Uncovering Murder Plot.' Lead story *and* a picture. I'm sending a copy to my mother. And my ex—it's a good picture."

"Send me one, too," I said.

"Already in the mail. You think she'll ever wash up?"

"It could happen," I said. "I almost hope it doesn't."

"How come?"

"She should rest." I patted the empty air. "Rest."

"One thing I should tell you before you read the story. That reporter really played it up about me, like I solved the damned thing. I really didn't try to take the credit. Just wanted you to know."

"It doesn't matter to me."

"You're the one who cracked the conspiracy."

"Those work out so seldom, you wonder why people persist in conspiring."

"Maybe that should be your specialty. That Kennedy thing still troubles a lot of people."

"Have you ever been to Dallas? There's a big white X on the road where he was shot. During breaks in traffic, tourists run over from the grassy knoll and pose on it for a picture."

"You sound surprised."

"It's counterintuitive," I admitted. "You'd think somebody in my line of work would be more accustomed to the weirdness of people."

Silence, as if she had run out of things to say. It was the reason for mine anyway.

"Anyway," she said.

I looked over at Archie. His eyes were closed. I closed mine.

"You going to keep your bargain with me, Ragman?" she asked.

"Bargain?"

"Dinner in exchange for my cracking your case for you."

"Oh. That bargain."

"Knoxville, Savannah, or somewhere in between?"

"Well, that wouldn't be right, you driving all the way to Knoxville so I can treat you to dinner."

"I know this great little place not far from the beach. You like French food?"

"Love the fries."

"Their foie gras is to *die* for."

"Well. *Très magnifique*."

"So how about next week? Friday."

"Oh. Friday."

"You're busy Friday."

"Don't know, but I'm sure I am. Fridays are bad in general. So much mopping up from the rest of the week."

"Saturday."

"This Saturday?"

"Or next Saturday. Either Saturday."

"I'd have to find a sitter."

"You have a kid?"

"I have a dog."

"That's right. Artimus."

"Archie."

"Artimus sounds more like a detective's dog."

"Well, he's about two, and that would be like renaming your fourteen-year-old. Confusing."

"Bring him along."

"The restaurant allows pets?"

"Ruzak, they're French."

"Maybe someplace in between would be best," I said. "Neutral territory."

"What, we're signing an armistice? Ruzak, you have no intention of paying me back, have you?"

"I want to pay you back."

"It's just dinner, and you won't be drinking."

"I won't?"

"I've seen you when you've been drinking."

"Right. Plus, I have to drive back."

"Pessimist."

"You're the one who said 'just dinner.' But it's funny you said that. All my life I've thought of myself as the opposite."

We hung up without resolving anything. I looked at my watch. Five after seven: the *Wheel of Fortune* hour. Archie's eyes were still closed. The atmosphere was rich with the odor of his bowels. I had switched dog foods four times, trying to resolve his flatulence problems, all to no avail. Putin always made me think of the fart euphemism, *poot. Maybe I should rename him Vladimir,* I thought.

"You know, Arch, subtract a couple of inches and add a few pounds, and Vanna White would be a dead ringer for Katrina Bates."

The name had come up recently—on my caller ID. For a single horrible, irrational second, I thought it would be her voice on the other end. Of course it wasn't.

"We're getting back together," Tom Bates had said.

"You and Kinsey?"

"No, me and Katrina. Come on, Ruzak. Why do you do that?"

"That's a question I often ask myself," I said. "Why I lack that internal editing function most people take for granted."

"Well, you're not fooling me. What's puzzling is most of us want others to think we're *smarter* than we really are."

"Maybe it's a strategy to lower expectations because as an only child I had undue burdens placed upon me."

He laughed. "I can picture you as a child."

What the hell did that mean? I said, "Well, that's terrific. She's a nice girl."

"She distrusted my motives," he said without a hint of irony. "She thought I only asked her to marry me because she was pregnant. She thought I viewed her as a baby-delivery system, not a person I wanted to spend the rest of my life with."

"Sort of like Katrina," I said.

"See? This proves my point about you."

"Evidence," I said. "Not proof."

"That's not the reason for my call," he said.

"You want to thank me for saving your life."

"See? You *are* capable of it."

"Maybe your life wouldn't have needed saving if you had been faithful to your wife."

"I know where this is going."

"Well, if anybody would . . ."

"It's my fault. If not for my little adventures, Katrina would still be alive."

"'Little adventures.' I like that, Tom. Like skydiving or snorkeling on the Great Barrier Reef."

"The problem with that kind of thinking, Ted, is that you never reach the end of it, like the value of *pi*."

"That's a poor analogy," I said. "It's more like the butterfly effect."

"Oh." He laughed. "*You're* going to lecture *me* about chaos theory."

"Tom, I wouldn't dream of lecturing a brick wall, much less a brainiac like you. I'm just the thick sap who nabbed your wife's killer."

"Maybe it's Alistair's fault for fucking the baby-sitter thirty years ago."

"Violin tutor."

"Whatever. You know what I mean."

"We've drifted a far piece from 'thank you.'"

"Something else," he said. "We're holding a memorial service for Kat this Sunday on Tybee. At sunset. Wanted you to know."

"Okay," I said. "Now I know."

Sun fading in a violet sky (Walter Hinton was an idiot), I sat on my sofa, silent cell phone in one hand, television remote in the other, both delivery systems of things I had no stomach for at that moment. I had important stuff to do. Walk Archie. Feed him. Feed me. Put him to bed. Put myself to bed. *Animal Cops* came on at nine. I was fairly certain there would be no segment featuring a Border collie's plot to frame its owners for murder. Animals are like us, only better. Maybe not better, just luckier, less burdened by memory and guilt.

There was some leftover pizza in the fridge—spinach deep-dish, my favorite—and some lettuce I should eat before it went bad. *What the heck is foie gras?* I wondered. *Isn't that like duck guts or something?* Her lips had tasted salty from the crackers, sweet from the wine, and when she laughed, her mouth didn't open too wide like a lot of women's, but her tongue felt fat as a sausage in my mouth and the texture was like fine sandpaper or the roughness of a cat's. I tried to remember what her hair had smelled like. Felicia's had a fruity smell, like peaches, and her legs were better; I had never seen better legs in real life, nicely toned from years working as a waitress. And then there were those knees.

"Not you. Not you," I'd said to Melody after my boorish pass. Felicia had said the same to me during another man's boorish pass: "Not you." And Meredith, that very day: "It's not you." It could have been the leitmotiv of the entire affair, from the moment Katrina Bates brought the curtain up on this absurd little morality play. *Not you, not you.* If she or Tom or even her dad back when she was a twelve-year-old little girl, walking in on something no little girl should ever walk in on, had said "Yes, you" none of it would have happened. The one person who did say "Yes, you"—a big homely girl with a big ugly crush on a poor man's George Clooney—made it possible. I had told Alistair Lynch it revolved around connection; actually, it was connection's opposite, the failure to connect, the longing to fill something that perhaps, ultimately, tragically, could not be filled. It wasn't about sex, she'd told me on our first meeting. Sitting on my sofa, remote in one hand, cell phone in the other, I realized it wasn't about revenge, either. It was about those damn monkeys. The need to be needed, the desire to be desired, and the absurd lengths we are willing to go to fill that hole, not to feel so damn empty and alone, to feel important to someone or something, to be connected. *Not you. Not you.*

I struggled to maintain a grip on myself, and lost. There are some cognitive paths you simply should not traverse, and I had wandered off, once again, into the thickets; I had stripped off my clothes, once again, and dived naked into the crashing surf, where all sorts of hidden, alien creatures resided, the most benign of which might sting me, and where the most malignant might eat me. My chest heaved. I fought for breath. Katrina went down with arms outstretched reaching for her killer. *Not you,* says Dresden Falks. *Not you.*

Caught in a riptide, I struggled to reach the surface as the waves roiled around my flailing limbs. I cried for help, but seawater filled my mouth as I reached, as I reached, reached, but no one was above me to grab my outstretched hand.

I don't know how long I sat there, drowning on my sofa, being pulled slowly, inexorably down, every muscle and sinew taut as piano wire, before I felt his warmth on my thigh, the warmth that's born of another living thing. I didn't hear the *clickety-click* of his nails on the hardwood or the pant of his breath. I wasn't aware he had come to me until I looked down and saw his head resting on my leg, saw his soft, sad brown eyes through the watery prism of my own. The remote slipped from my fingers and I placed my empty hand upon him. His eyes never left my face and, out of my peripheral vision, I saw the tip of his tail give the slightest of twitches.

Yes, you.

CURTAIN SLOWLY FALLS

ACKNOWLEDGMENTS

Thanks to all the good people at Thomas Dunne Books, particularly my editor, Marcia Markland, and Diana Szu.

Special thanks to my good friend and agent, Brian DeFiore, possessor of the best laugh I have ever heard.

Thanks to Elbert Reed for all his help over the years. And thanks to Josh for *Celtic*.

And Sandy, from whom I have learned so much, to whom I owe so much, and with whom I have shared so much, thank you. Yes, you.